I0655504

Chicago Police Detective Samantha Dahill must fight her inner demons in order to bring a sadistic serial killer to justice while discovering the horror of waking up in bed with the gentle seduction from this terrifying stranger's hands.

Will she be able to discover the killer and stop him before he tires of his bedroom games and decides to end her life as well?

"2012 was 50 Shades - this year is Dead Envy!"

"This isn't your grandmothers type of romance story, not your mother's type either. This isn't even your older sister's type of romance story. Very sexy."

"A cross between Silvia Day and Dashiell Hammett. Refreshing and different."

DEAD ENVY

CHRISSY DEKER

wordsworthwhile publishing

This novel is a work of fiction. All of the characters, names, places and events are used fictitiously and are products of the authors imagination. Any resemblance to actual events or people, living or dead, is purely coincidental.

DEAD ENVY

Copyright © 2013 Chrissy Deker. All rights reserved.
ISBN 978-0-9920374-2-0
http://www.chrissydeker.com

All rights reserved. No part of this book may be reproduced in any manner or form whatsoever, except for brief quotations for articles or reviews, without written permission from the author.

wordsworthwhile publishing
http://www.wordsworthwhilepublishing.com
http://www.dead-envy.com

wordsworthwhile publishing edition / September 2013

ISBN 978-0-9920374-2-0

9 780992 037420

Thank you to my fabulous editor …

DEAD ENVY

chapter one

She wasn't paying attention as she closed the door ... a hand reached out and clamped over her mouth. Her newspaper dropped to the floor.

She tried to scream, but it was no use. Samantha collapsed.

She awoke. How long? It only took her seconds to realize she couldn't see because she was blindfolded. Some sort of mask that didn't trap her eyes.

All her limbs seemed strapped down - even her head and torso. She couldn't move. Panic rose. Fear.

What the hell ... what's just happened here, she thought. I can't move ... I can't see ... fuck ... fuck ... I'm panicking here ... wait ... have to get control ... take a deep breath ... wait ... wait where am I? I know that smell ... geez that's my perfume ... I'm in my own damn house ... what the hell just happened ... Who's doing this?

She knew she was strapped to her own bed. Strapped down with her arms and legs spread apart. Nothing hurt, but she couldn't move.

Damn, my gun is in the drawer down-stairs, she thought. Useless. Me and my gun. What the hell am I going to do?

Samantha lay quietly, trying to listen to the room. Nothing.

She tried to kick out but couldn't move her legs. She tried to pull with her arms, nothing. Her body was completely immo-bilized, effectively stopping her from doing anything but waiting.

God damn it, she thought, some cop, not so tough now am I. Fear. A tear slid down her cheek.

Silence.

Then she heard sounds. Someone quietly walking around the room. She held her breath.

Sam couldn't move ... she didn't want to move. Scared ... very scared.

She wanted the person to go away. Go away and let Thomas find her. Save her. It would be a few days before he would be back. Damn business trip. Days ... She could last.

Just lay here and be quiet, she thought ... as long as no one touches me.

She felt chilled and realized she was tied to the bed naked. Suddenly she felt embar-rassed. She didn't know why. Who was watching her? Who was in the room?

Bastard ... let me go you bastard, she thought still holding her breath. She struggled.

Her breath escaped with panic as her right thigh was lightly brushed. The explosion of touch clamped her lower body rigid as her upper body tried to breath.

Holy hell … what's going on? Who is this, she thought? Oh God, how do I stop this?

She tried to breath as slowly as she dared, not making a sound.

Noises ... sounds of a case being opened, a zipper. Then soft sounds, material. Sudden smell of leather.

Sounds of movement. Someone suddenly standing over her breathing. The smell of mouthwash and aftershave or cologne. Strong smells.

Where was Thomas? she wondered. Why did he have to go on that business trip? Why couldn't he be here? Who is this? How did they get in? Thomas left just minutes before I opened the front door to get the paper. How did this bastard get me? How did I let that happen?

Focus girl, she told herself. Pay attention. What am I hearing? What am I smelling? Remember everything. If this bastard wanted you dead, you would be. What does he want? Unless it's just ... no can't think like that. Okay just concentrate. Must stop this bastard.

Smells. Cologne. Must be a man ... strong cologne smells. Men's cologne. Couldn't be a woman could it? I have never been with a woman, she thought. Fuck, fuck, fuck what's going on here?

Sounds. Almost nothing, she thought. Very quiet. Waiting ... don't panic, it won't help. Focus.

The stereo was turned on and a CD slipped into the player. Music slowly began to breath in and out, filling the room. Slowly replacing every bit of air in the room. Filling all space with an exotic sound. Filling her head.

Eastern? Middle Eastern? she wondered. Very exotic.

Sound of a match being lit, very close to her left ear. She sucked air quickly. The match was moved away. The smells of scented candles danced inside her nose.

What does my room look like in candle-light? she thought. I've never seen that. What time is it? Is it dark?

She almost began to relax. The exotic music ... the erotic smells.

Focus! she thought. You have to re-member everything about this guy.

Sam jumped inside her restraints. A soft touch. A feather or a brush. It stroked her left leg from top to bottom. It stopped at her foot. Then reversed upward until her left breast.

This can't be happening, she thought, this has to stop. What's he doing to me?

She opened her mouth, "please ..." was all she said.

What the hell was that? she wondered. Was that begging? It sounded like begging, didn't it? Why am I begging? This can't be happening. Stop. Stop. Stop.

The feather or brush circled her right breast.

"Oh God", she sighed.

Between her legs became moist. More embarrassment.

The bastard, she thought. This isn't supposed to feel good ... I can't let this feel good.

Her body betrayed her.

A gloved hand rubbed and massaged her left nipple. Strong and just a hint of pain. A quiet smooth stroke of the hand down the right side of her neck.

As she sighed again, something pressed against her half open mouth. She relaxed and opened. Her mouth was full before she reacted. It felt like hard rubber.

Now she had even lost her chance to speak. Her chance to cry out for help.

Where are you Thomas? she wondered.

The gloved hand touched her face. Slowly, softly. First her left cheek, then her right cheek and down to her chin. A feather like kiss to the tip of her nose. Softly, sensually. Strong smells of leather from the soft gloves, mixed with aftershave and cologne. Beautiful smells. Another beautiful kiss - light. A tongue rolled across her left cheek.

She felt his clothes on her skin. Warm, soft clothes.

She couldn't stop this person ... even if she wanted to. She knew it. And he knew it. He took his time. He was in no hurry. He kissed her forehead two times lightly.

She felt her captor lower himself down to the edge of the bed and run his hands through her hair. He was stroking her hair, fingers out, like a comb. A human comb.

He blew so lightly, almost kissing her, starting behind her left ear and moving down her neck to her chest. He circled her breasts and massaged each with cupped hands. Her nipples became hard and tingling. His touch was electrifying, sending waves of mind numbing shocks throughout her body, her nerves exploding in her head.

She had never experienced anything like this before, but she knew her body was on fire. She wasn't controlling anything, her body was controlling her now.

She felt so exposed, so helpless ... but so alive. So very alive.

The gloved hand moved down to her stomach. Fingers began to circle. They found her navel. And kept circling. In no rush. Fingers with no certain destination in mind ... only a journey. A highly-charged wandering journey. Where every touch, every stroke, every brush was sending electrical charges throughout her body.

His hands never stopped moving. The smooth, warm and soft touch of leather brushing against her skin left enormous haunting feelings of desire inside her core. She couldn't understand how he could make her entire body feel so in tune, so fantastic as a whole instrument for his teasing pleasure.

The loud, exotic music. The smooth, hot, scented candles. A world created where she could only hear and smell. She could not move. She could not see or speak. She could not think.

She could not help but relax and breath deep through her nose. The fingers kept circling and her whole body began to waver and deep rushes of feelings washed through her.

She felt her captor shift on the edge of the bed. His hands withdrew. He stood up and moved away.

She quietly began to weep.

chapter two

Sam only wept briefly, but that was enough. She felt relieved.

She heard him return and felt him sit on the edge of the bed again.

What the hell is he going to do to me now? she wondered. Why was he taking so long? Where is this all going? Hands that have given me such exquisite pleasure, can they hurt me too? What is he doing? He still has all his clothes on. I feel so exposed. What's he doing now? Has he finished toying with me? Is he going to rape me now? Her mind was racing.

He laid his hand flat on her crotch and began to circle. The lower half of her body began to spasm. She felt so helpless but still so energized. She knew she was under her body's control and her body was under his spell. He was controlling everything.

Even her orgasms.

The first caught her by surprise. She could tell she was building slowly, but she came suddenly and without a fight. Body jolting as the soft leather fingers moved down to her legs. They brushed up and down, from thigh to shin and back ... slowly. They caressed the tops of her feet as she shook with spasms of ecstasy against her bindings.

"Oh fuck", she spoke through her gag.

Her mind drifted. She thought of Thomas. What am I am going to do? Have I betrayed him? Where is he, damn him … what is he doing right at this moment. On the plane? Is he even there yet? What time is it? He's probably in some boring meeting. Oh Thomas … my Thomas … you're always there for me. Where are you now?

She had always thought of Thomas as one of the best-looking men she had ever met. And he had such a commanding presence. Yet he was still so care free. She wondered how could he always be so care free? Nothing ever seemed to worry him or ever get to him. Not that she was complaining. She loved Thomas and knew she always would. Till death does you - or whatever it was …

She and Thomas had never really ventured far from the missionary position, when they would finally get to have sex. It was not often it seemed. But she felt safe. Safe and secure laying under him while he was inside her. She liked it when he came inside her, she loved the feeling deep inside. But then she always felt that she had to get up quickly to pee and empty his sperm out.

She never really worried too much about not having many orgasms herself. She had always read about those ladies who thought it was the end of the world when they didn't come. But for her she felt that the closeness and companionship during sex was the most important thing. She didn't need orgasms for that did she?

Sam didn't feel justified in demanding she have her own pleasure. It seemed like it was too much trouble and bother for their lifestyle. There wasn't time for such things, was there? She just wanted Thomas to come and secretly she felt that Thomas thought the same way. But she would never discuss it with him and since he never asked, she was fairly sure he didn't really think about her pleasure either.

And her mother instilled the good old fashioned thoughts about sex - to be a good wife, as they say. Let your husband come and you just lay there and worry about his pleasure. If your orgasm isn't going to improve his experience or speed his orgasm up, then why bother.

Neither of them seemed to need sex all that much. She worked hard at her job everyday. He seemed to work hard all the time.

They had work instead of sex. He never showed his need for it. Or his liking of it, did he?

Was he normal? Was she normal?

Or maybe he was finding pleasure some other ways? she wondered.

She had never really been all that comfortable with pleasing herself by masturbating. She had only tried it a few times in her life but had always felt so guilty and even a little silly each time.

Fuck, she thought, where is Thomas when I really need him? Quick Thomas hand me my gun and I'll get this guy off me.

She felt so exposed, so humiliated, betrayed by her body for having had an orgasm.

How could she help it, she thought. Those amazing hands inside the soft gloves, the cologne, her nakedness, her helplessness. She shouldn't have come.

Laying naked with someone unknown stroking her body ... she felt so alone.

Something was dragging slowly up her left leg. Something soft. Like a silk tie or silk glove. Smooth material ... dragging upward.

The material slowed as it reached her vagina. Legs apart, fully exposed, the material slowly dragged across her clitoris and lower belly. It slowly moved up ... stopped ... and dragged down over her clit again. And again ... up ... down ... up ... down.

God ... this is heaven, her thoughts raced. This ... is ... heaven! Don't ... stop!

She let go ... she felt like time had stopped.

She shook hard as she came for the second time. Her breath became a groan. Her mind exploded with passionate and colorful sensations like fireworks. Her highly charged inner core pulsed with the strength of her orgasm. She had trouble falling back to normal.

She took a slow deep breath.

She began to think. What if she never experiences all this pleasure again? She knew she couldn't explain any of this to anyone. How could she ever put this to words or tell anyone how much she liked it?

The body above her shifted on the bed. She felt a pull on her middle finger of her left hand. It was gently bent over and a ring slipped over her nail.

What the hell? she thought.

Silence. She drifted off.

chapter three

She awoke. How long was she out she wondered?

She was hungry. She was drained. And yet she still felt so horny.

She still couldn't move, getting stiff. She tried different things. Nothing ... no movement possible.

Where was he? she wondered.

Wait ... she remembered ... what was the ring? She straightened her finger and her left hand came free.

She felt relief ... she removed the mask from her eyes. It was a leather mask obviously made for the sex trade - bdsm - something to sensually blind a captive.

Her bedroom seemed slightly strange at first. Off color somehow. She blinked. She pulled on the strap and removed her gag.

Breath deep ... again ... breath again, her mind was telling her. Relief. Yes it really is my room. Safe again in my room. Tied down, but safe. No one around.

She untied her right hand and leaned forward to untie the ribbons across her body and around her ankles. The ribbons had been tied in bows not knots so they weren't difficult to undo. Plus her left hand had been attached with some sort of clip. A quick release that opened when she straightened her finger. Obviously, she was supposed to get away. She was to live another day.

She looked at her belly. Still felt the hand on her nipple and the silk on her clit. God ... still horny. She placed her right fingers down on her clit. She wanted more ... it had stopped too soon.

Have to masturbate?

NO ... she thought. What am I doing ... I've been violated. Call the station - idiot!

She found her robe on the floor and covered herself. She blew out the candles and turned off the stereo. She ran down the stairs to find her cell phone. The ringing wouldn't stop.

"Hello," she said quietly.

"Hey there partner."

Robert.

"Oh, Robert," was all she could sigh, "please ..."

"What's wrong?" Robert perked up.

"Just ..."

"Don't move kiddo, I'm on my way." He hung up.

She walked into the kitchen and sat at the table. It wasn't quite dark outside yet.

The clock on the stove read 5:34 p.m. Okay, she thought, I must have been upstairs, tied to the bed for at least what, five or six hours? Thomas had left sometime just before noon. Today? Yesterday? What happened?

What can I tell Robert? He'll go ballistic. His little partner ... raped ... in her own bedroom ... in her own bed. She couldn't think properly.

Wait a minute, she was confused. She wasn't raped was she? Yes, she was violated, but not raped. The guy just rubbed her legs a couple of times and ran a glove across her clit for a few strokes. She was the one who broke down and came twice.

Fuck, what to say to Robert? she worried. "He came, he touched, and I came ... twice." Robert will go ballistic.

Horny, she touched herself again. She spread her fingers and rubbed her right hand across her clit. It felt so good. She opened her legs more.

Wait, she thought, look around ... can anyone see in? Can the neighbors see past the trees in the back yard?

Circle ... circle ... circle the fingers. Just like his feather did around her nipple and his hand did around her navel.

She felt totally exposed. Even now. Sitting in her own kitchen. Legs reaching apart ... robe half off at the shoulders ... right hand rubbing her clit ... left hand rolling a nipple between her fingers. She squeezed. Harder.

She started to rub hard back and forth. Only one thought, one memory, those amazing hands.

Suddenly the guilt and shame hit her hard again. She stopped, She pulled her robe closed.

Silly woman, she thought, normal girls don't do that sort of thing.

Doorbell! Damn ... the choice over - the moment was gone.

She opened the front door.

"Hey Robert," she smiled. She led him into the kitchen. He sat where she had been rubbing herself moments before.

If only he knew, she thought. What would he say? His partner, his trusted partner ... masturbating in the kitchen. In the very chair he was sitting on. Would he like to see ... would he watch? Would he be interested?

Robert ... the funny soul, she thought. He always struck her as not really worrying about girls and sex, but you never know.

The old saying - it's the quiet ones that you have to worry about.

She turned to make coffee.

"So what the hell happened?" he asked.

"What do you mean?" she asked.

"What's the pair of panties doing on your front stairs?"

"What?" She ran to the front door.

God, what about the neighbors! she was thinking as she ran. No one around. Pick them up ... get the hell back inside quick ... before anyone sees. And they are one of my favorite pairs too.

What the fuck? she questioned herself. She definitely hadn't been dreaming earlier, but she knew that. She didn't need to be reminded. Then why were her panties out in the front? A sign? A warning? Of what? Would he be back?

"Shit," she crossed by the stairs. She was almost feeling moist again looking upstairs. She shoved the panties deep into her pocket.

"Will he be back?" she whispered as she went back to the kitchen to join Robert.

"So?" he asked. "You sounded funny when I called. Is everything okay?"

She started in, telling him a rambling story about one of the upstairs windows getting stuck and the wind gusting badly

before she finally got it closed. Her clothes
were swirling around the room and one
article must have actually made it out the
window and dropped onto the front steps.

Robert stood up, leaned against the
counter. He stared at her as if he knew she
was drunk or stoned or something.

Change the subject, she thought. Go
back to making coffee.

"So how was the interrogation today?"
she asked.

"You mean the phone call with Cummings?" he asked.

"Well yes."

"Rotten, what a waste of time." he hesitated. "Smug bastard ... he still denies that
he killed her. Stubborn shit. And I can't get
him to even admit that he and Connie were
intimate."

"We have to find a way," she said.

"Look," he said, "you don't still feel
guilty about Connie do you? You know you
couldn't have done a thing about it ... I
keep telling you, there is absolutely no way
you could have known what Cummings
was going to do to her. No one would have
known."

"Well I should have," she said. "I talked
to him almost everyday. He had me so

fooled, I just feel awful that I had no idea he was planning on killing her."

"Get some sleep kid," he said. "You look terrible."

If only you knew, she thought.

"If you're making that coffee for me and you feel okay now, I'd just as soon go home. We can go through this stuff tomorrow, sleep on it will yah ..."

"Missing your football?" She asked.

He just stared at her again.

"Okay, thank you Robert, for coming over ... it was nothing ... I just need ... in a bit ... I'm sorry."

"Hey, no prob kid." He hugged her.

"Just take care," he said. "And quit blaming yourself." He seemed in a real hurry to hit the door. "See you in the morning ..."

Gone. Alone again.

Did she smell? Could he smell her? Her orgasms. Is that why he left so quickly? She flushed. She felt so guilty for her earlier pleasure.

She checked to make sure she hadn't turned the coffee on and that the doors were secure. She went upstairs to have a shower.

What the hell was she going to tell Thomas when he got home?

chapter four

Loud Bells, confusion! Chaos!

Fucking alarm clock. Fucking Monday mornings. Always too early.

She looked around her room. The ribbons were still tied to the bed. The feather lay on the floor, the blindfold and mouth gag lay by her pillow. A bright, red silk scarf draped across the chair.

Must have been his, she thought, because it isn't mine.

She had to go to work. The Anderson case. Today was the day when her and Robert had an appointment for an initial interview with Marshal Anderson, Connie's husband. The poor guy who found his wife kneeling naked and dead, tied up by their bed with a couple of belts around her wrists and neck. She had a pair of her own panty hose shoved deep down her throat while her mouth was held open by a mouth gag and her eyes were covered with a mask. Ghastly, messy murder, but just another day it seemed for Samantha and Robert. They had to try to find the truth of what really happened to Connie. The real ugly truth.

Sam knew Connie and Marshal but not very well. She had met them both a few times at neighborhood barbecues and block parties. But she had dealt with Barry Cummings quite a bit lately. Her and Thomas had hired Barry to refinish their kitchen. Help local trades, Thomas had said at the time. Help local crazy man, Sam realized now.

Damn, she thought. A day off would be nice. I haven't been able to sleep much. Feels like I only got an hour of sleep. Day off ... no office ... no Robert ... no Thomas. No one and nothing to do. Nothing but memories. His smells, his gloves, his touch on my stomach, on my nipple. The scarf!

She reached over with her left hand and dragged the scarf across her belly. She wanted to touch herself more but felt the guilt and shame again.

Fucking feelings, she thought, always feeling ridiculous doing something that's supposed to come naturally.

She got out of bed to pee and shower.

Forty minutes later, if anyone had been paying attention to her that morning, they would have noticed when she left to go to the office. She was wearing a bright, red scarf that didn't really match her burgundy outfit so well.

When she arrived at the precinct she walked quickly to her desk and sat down. She had left the scarf in her car, not knowing who gave it to her. She had suddenly become very self conscious wearing it.

The squad room was a rather large room with fifteen foot ceilings. Although the building was supposedly built in the modern era, it still seemed like the room itself was in the architectural style of old. Really old. The wood running around the outside walls had the shade of medium brown that could have come from many years of layered cigarette smoke. Nowadays of course, no one smoked inside the room, but Sam had heard stories years ago of the air being so thick you couldn't see the far walls.

The desks were made of metal and medium brown wood. They looked tired and well used, stories could be told from each stain and broken corner. They sat in pairs spread throughout the room as if the department wanted everyone to know that they needed all the room that they'd been given.

The chairs had seen better days as well. Each had worn down in various areas so it appeared to be a custom fit to a particular detective, but in actuality they just hurt everyone in different places.

Monday morning was a little quiet. Robert walked in just minutes after Sam.

"So you ready to go?" he asked. "I was hoping we'd be able to stop for a coffee on the way."

"Sounds good," she answered.

They hit the closest Starbucks and sat at a table in the middle of the room.

"So tell me," Robert said, "last night you seemed really wired, is everything okay?"

"Yes of course! I've just been going through a few things lately, I'll be fine."

"Well whatever it is partner," he said, "you know you can talk to me about it alright. That's what partners do okay?"

"Sure."

"So anyway, what do you think of Marshall Anderson?"

"He seems to be a nice enough guy. I don't really know him very well but he's polite enough to me and Thomas whenever we've seen him."

"Does he come across as a killer? Does it seem like it's possible that he killed his wife?"

"I think that we are all capable of killing at some point if we have to," Sam said, "or are really angry enough ... maybe even crazy enough. I don't know."

"Just wondered about your impressions, that's all. You know your woman's intuition."

Huh, she thought, my intuition? You want my woman's intuition when I can't even figure out who had me in bed yesterday and turned my world upside down. There's a laugh. Pathetic.

"Well he seems okay to me, but you never know do you?"

"You ready to go talk to Marshall? Robert asked.

"Let's go get it over with," Sam answered.

chapter five

"Hey what are these marks?" Axel pointed to Sam's wrists. He was standing behind her ready to grab the barbells as she was attempting to do another bench press of 150 pounds.

Sam flushed. "Nothing." She was shocked. She had completely forgotten about any of the marks on her body.

Axel Blaine, her personal trainer, was the first one to see much of her body since the event. That's what she called it, the event. She hated to think of it as anything specific ... The rape ... The encounter ... The incredible day?

And now she had to worry about the marks on her body. She looked around the gym and wondered if anyone else had seen the marks.

Fuck. How long will they still show? she wondered.

They were clearly visible around her wrists but only from close up.

Shit, she thought, should've worn sweatbands.

Luckily her socks mostly covered the marks around her ankles.

"It looks like you and your husband have been into the naughty chest huh?" Axel said. "you had some fun trying bondage? Hands tied behind your back or something?"

"Oh shit no," Sam said still flushed with embarrassment, "it's not like that at all. Thomas and I are not into that kind of thing."

"Hey I'm not judging you Samantha, I don't care what you and your husband do for fun."

"I would never be caught doing any of that kinky stuff," she said.

"Ah relax Sam," he said, "I don't care ... I was just asking that's all."

She placed the bar back on the rack and sat up. Then she pulled up both socks.

How could she explain? Her and Thomas had never talked about that kind of thing. Her and Thomas had never really even talked about sex together. They just kind of made it work without ever thinking about it. She wasn't even comfortable thinking about it. She wouldn't even know how to bring up a conversation like that with Thomas. Her deep desires.

"Although I don't know what husband wouldn't want to tie this up," Axel said as he rubbed her shoulders, "and then fuck your brains out."

"Shut up!" Sam punched him in the arm.

"Well I've got to tell you, you have done a phenomenal job getting back into shape this year. You look really lean and mean. You look absolutely terrific."

"Thanks," Sam said, "but I don't really think that's true. I just don't want to get injured again like last year."

"No I'm serious," he said, "you've really toned up."

"Well you're the first person to notice."

"Really? I can't imagine that … Thomas must tell you stuff like that all the time."

"I don't think he finds that kind of stuff all that important," Sam said.

"God, and here I was thinking all this time he's been trying to jump you every moment of every day. I know I would be." He smiled.

"Oh give it a rest Axel, you're just looking for a bigger tip," Sam laughed.

But she thought he was nuts, she thought she looked the same as she always did.

chapter six

Friday evening Thomas had just finishing hanging a photo in the living room when Sam walked in after work.

"Hey honey," he said, "what do you think?"

The photo he had hung was one he had taken of Sam last summer when they were out camping. The photo showed her sitting in a camping chair with no clothes on. Not a stitch. Naked. Although she wasn't wearing anything, you couldn't really see anything too revealing by the position she was sitting in.

"You can't leave that up," she said. It still amazed her that he had been able to talk her into posing that way. What the hell was she thinking at the time?

"Why not," Thomas said, "it is one of my all time favorite photos of you … you're beautiful."

"Thomas," she said, "what will people think if you leave that up …"

"What, that I'm the luckiest guy to be married to such a beautiful woman?"

"You know what I mean."

"Oh Samantha Dahill - you have to learn to loosen up!" said Thomas. "Speaking of which, I hope you didn't forget that we are out tonight."

"No," she said, "I didn't forget. I was just hoping you had."

"No way, I've been looking forward to this all week," he said. "You have an hour and then we have to go."

An hour or so later, Sam came out of the bedroom and was grabbed by Thomas. He threw his arm around her waist and spun her into his grasp.

"My God you look stunning," he said. He nuzzled her neck and kissed it several times with light little kisses. He reached behind her and fumbled with the zipper of her dress.

"Hey what are you doing?" she asked. She stepped back and reached around and pulled his hand away. "I just spent half an hour getting into this thing."

"Ah come on Sam," he said "how about a little fun before we go."

"Ah come on Thomas," she mocked, "we're late." She turned and went down the stairs.

And they were out the door to a formal cocktail party being held across the street.

chapter seven

The following Tuesday night Sam decided to take a bath. Another long day at the precinct had forced her to miss dinner. She didn't get home until after nine and she had stopped on the way to pick up a burger. She needed the down time just to refuel herself, that's what she told Thomas.

But she had a hard time convincing herself to relax as she lay in the tub thinking about the case. Why would he murder Connie?

She was a little startled when Thomas brought in two glasses of wine.

"Surprise," he said and handed her a glass. "Thought you might want some to unwind."

"Thanks, that was very thoughtful honey."

"Hey," he smiled and sat down on the edge of the tub, "always your humble servant madam."

"Yah right," she said, "you're just looking for a little action."

"So how is everything going at the office?" Thomas asked.

"Fine, it's just this murder case. It's like, you know, really bringing me down. Poor Connie."

"I'll say, nobody can stop talking about it around here. Geez, the other night at Yvonne and Malcolm's party everyone I talked to wanted to know if you had solved the case yet and caught the bastard."

"I know and no we haven't got any hard evidence yet. We think Barry did it but we haven't got any proof," Sam said.

"Just think," Thomas said, "what kind of torture he put Connie through while she was dying. My God, it would have been horrible."

They drank their wine in silence. After Sam had finished her glass, Thomas went back into the kitchen and brought back the bottle. He refilled her glass and began lightly brushing her head and neck as she sipped her wine and thought more about Connie.

"I want you to relax Sam," Thomas said. "Forget about everything."

"So ..." she answered.

He took her glass and placed them both on the counter. He leaned forward and kissed her. She responded and their mouths opened and explored each other without limits. His tongue rolled around hers as she sucked him in. She loved it when his tongue went deep into her mouth, she would suck as if trying to get him off.

Thomas reached down and circled her left breast. His hand easily gliding over her slippery wet skin. He reached over and squeezed her right nipple lightly and circled both breasts.

He stopped kissing her mouth but leaned in and kissed her neck and behind her ears. She could feel between her legs start to respond as she leaned back resting her head. She moved her knees apart slightly and braced her feet against the edge of the tub.

Thomas moved one hand down to her stomach and rubbed her below the water. He slowly moved toward her vagina in a long slow circling motion. She could hear herself moaning in anticipation.

But then he stopped moving down and instead grabbed her right hand. He straightened her fingers under the water and pushed her hand down between her legs. He held her middle finger as he circled her clit using her hand as a pleasure toy.

"There," he said, "how does that feel?"

"Ummmmm," was all she could say.

He kissed her mouth again and continued masturbating her with her own hand. A moment later he let go of her hand and moved up to her breasts.

She stopped moving her hand and sat up.

"I'm sorry I just can't, not right now," she said.

"Oh Sam," he said, "you've got to learn to let go ... not worry about things so much."

"I know," she said, "I'm sorry."

"Enjoy life, it's fast and it's quick."

"I know."

"And it's over before you know it."

"I know."

"And it's meant to be fun."

"I know."

"You've got to let go Sam." He picked up the glasses and left the bathroom.

"I'm sorry." she said but he was already gone.

She couldn't sleep all night, she just lay worried while Thomas snored lightly beside her.

chapter eight

Wednesday over dinner Thomas announced that he had to go to Washington for the week. He was leaving Sunday morning.

A rush of memories! She began to weep silently. Thomas looked concerned and asked if anything was wrong. She assured him it was nothing as she ran upstairs.

She stood looking at herself in the mirror, crying. She had such mixed feelings. Horrible fucking mixed feelings. What could she do, what could she tell her husband? Nothing fatal had happened but everything had changed so much.

She was twenty eight years old, Samantha Lara Dahill, married for a little over three years, without kids and no real plans for them. A single child born into a standard middle class Catholic family and brought up with all the traditional Catholic guilt. Although for the last few years she had mostly let go of her religion.

And now she was a fairly sharp, witty, and up and coming detective with the Chicago Police Department. She had everything going for her. She was in great shape, not more than a pound or two overweight.

A great body-fat ratio or so she had been told by Axel. She had a slightly exotic look, at least that's what many people had told her, including Thomas. Maybe she thought, the result of having a Turkish mother and a white American father. Sam's hair was long and dark and spilled over her shoulders in natural curls.

And they seemed to be well enough off, although she never really knew. She made a good living but could never really tell how much money Thomas made. He was really rather secretive with his work. No amount of coaxing, inside the bedroom nor outside, would get him to loosen his tongue. She had learned a couple of years after they were married, that he worked for the government. But in what capacity, she had no idea.

And he hadn't even flinched at the costs of their fix-me-up house. An old brick detached house just down Addison from Wrigley Field where the Cubs played. They had purchased it together five years ago for what Sam thought was an outrageous sum, but it was just before the housing bust. And now with all the projects, tearing out the kitchen, redoing the living room, not once had he even brought up the costs.

When her and Thomas were married she had decided then that she was spoiled. She felt that Thomas had always been the only guy for her. He was tall and very handsome, his dark hair fell over his forehead in a sweeping tangle that he was always brushing out of his eyes. She loved it when he did that, it gave him such a schoolboy look. Her young, handsome schoolboy. He was almost a year younger than her but she always felt she looked so much older.

He was always so confident and knowing. He walked around with a slight smirk on his face like he knew some deep secret that no one else knew. But lately he sometimes seemed just too preoccupied. He was away a lot on business trips and would never discuss them with her. Some evenings when they were together, he would sit staring at her, but with a preoccupied look in his eyes.

But she loved him and he always seemed concerned that she had everything she needed.

He appeared at the bathroom door as she leaned against the counter, drying her eyes.

"Talk to me," he said. "Tell me what's wrong. Did something happen when I was away the last time?"

She stopped. Did he know? He couldn't or he would have said something. Had he talked to Robert? What the hell ... Robert didn't know anything.

Fuck ... tell? she wondered. Tell what? What happened? It was a long forgotten dream anyway. Not really forgotten, but faded. She still lay in bed the odd night when Thomas wasn't there, memories flooding through her. She remembered the touch. She had longed for those feelings again. She felt so alone. The memory of that touch made her realize how lonely she felt at times in the two weeks since that night. Two weeks with almost no sleep, or so it felt.

Fuck ... what to say? She was silent. She couldn't say anything. She thought, what could a person say? Hey buddy, your wife is being ravaged by a stranger in your own bed. Fuck. She couldn't say anything, he would go nuts. She was supposed to be this tough cop, she had to be able to handle it herself ... but she really didn't feel all that tough, she felt like a fraud. She came across on the outside as tough and competent but inside she knew the truth.

"No," she managed to get out. "Nothing happened. I'm just feeling a little overwhelmed with the work and everything. I just wish you didn't have to go."

"Well, it will all be over before you know it. And one of these weekends we can fly to New York and stay at the Plaza by Central Park. We'll go to dinner and one of those shows you like, if that's what you want."

"Since when did you want to go to a stage play ... or even out for dinner for that matter?"

"I will if you want me to," he said.

"Yah right," she said, "I'll believe it when I see it." In her head she was thinking, there is no fucking way he is going to want to go see a show.

"Come on," Thomas said, "let's go down and finish dinner. Can you promise not to be so dramatic?"

chapter nine

Morning came too early again. Damn alarm clock. Damn chaos in the head.

Thomas was leaving for Washington again. Mixed feelings. She should be all sad, shouldn't she? Somewhat ... but also excited. Would her secret lover be back? Oh she was feeling naughty. She wasn't raised to be like that. But hey, maybe this was her now ... a little sad ... a little excited. Confused.

It was like a familiar movie slowly playing in her head. She reached for the door as the hand went over her mouth. Same smells, same feeling of queasy euphoria. Same fall into darkness.

She woke in the same familiar position as well. Eyes dark but not forced closed, naked and tied to the four corners of her bed. Smells of leather and candles. And strong men's cologne. A brand not familiar. Not something Thomas would ever wear. Why didn't she notice that before?

Was this the same mask? she wondered. How could he have found it? I hid everything in my bottom drawer behind my sweaters. This couldn't be the same mask, could it? Where was he?

There was only silence. Silence and darkness.

Suddenly she felt his hands run up her left leg and she shivered violently. Fear gripped her again.

Who is he? What does he want? she asked herself. How is he knocking me out? What new drug am I being subjected to? Come on. Think. Remember everything. It will help at the trial. Sounds, smells and touch are the only senses left. I have to make them work hard for me. Focus. I have to remember. Oh God, what am I thinking ... touch ...

He was running his gloved fingers slowly over her breasts. She was wet already.

Ah fuck the courts, she thought, maybe I don't need to tell. She relaxed. Pinned down, felt up, guilt was slipping away.

I have no choice. I am stuck. This is so bad, so wrong, yet this is where I need to be, isn't it? Fuck I love it! she thought.

He shifted on the bed and the familiar smells of rubber and leather filled her nostrils again. She felt him place the gag in her mouth which she accepted this time willingly. Oh God I am in trouble, she thought. Thomas is going to kill me.

The exotic music filled the room as he started to play with her nipples again and she felt herself getting more and more wet. The desire was building inside her. She felt everything tighten up. She became hyper sensitive and her moist cunt was screaming to be touched. If only she could free her hand again, she would reach down herself and masturbate in front of this stranger. She started to think she wouldn't care who it was.

He slowly ran his gloves down her belly and down her legs. His touch was torture and he knew it. He was slowly torturing her to death. No, not death, but to heaven. She was building very slowly this time. The gloved hands were very slow and methodical in their torture.

Then she felt something sharp on her stomach. Something running around her stomach like a pen.

He was drawing on her! What the hell, she thought. He had to be. He was drawing on her body like it was paper. He drew circles and shapes around her stomach. He moved up to her breasts and drew around her nipples. There wasn't pain but instead strange and erotic feelings. The pen stroking around her nipples felt incredible.

He started down on her thighs and continued drawing circles round and round. It was driving her nuts. Just as he approached her crotch, he stopped. No, she thought. Through the gag she moaned. Begging again. Wanting more. She wanted to reach out, she wanted desperately to be touched.

Please touch my clit, she thought. Please.

She tried to move her hips up to his reach but forgot how well she was strapped down.

She waited for her controller. He was controlling her every move, every feeling. She waited as he shifted on the bed. She felt the pen dragging slowly across her lower belly. Inside she was yearning for relief, screaming at him, desire moving through every part of her body.

He placed his flat, gloved hand on her lower pubic bone and circled it slowly. She felt the rhythm of each of the circles as it changed, fast, slow, fast, slow. Her body felt like it was being tuned up for a performance. Her lower legs pulled at her restraints as they tensed up. Her breathing quickened and her inner core felt the now familiar build up of extreme pleasure. He moved his fingers down onto her clit and instantly she came. Wave after wave of relief. She poured out her tension from under her restraints. Her mind blown open with pleasure.

She wasn't used to these types of feelings. When Thomas and her made love her occasional orgasms were quick and precise. But this time her orgasm was wild and reckless. So much build up that she felt completely spent.

She lay quietly. She slowly brought her breathing back to normal. Her controller was slowly circling his gloved fingers around her pussy. They moved across her legs and followed by dragging the pen across her belly again and up to her stomach and breasts.

She tightened up again. Oh god this feels good, she thought. I want to be penetrated. I need you deep inside me. Please, whoever you are.

She felt so bad. Asking an unknown stranger to fuck her. What the hell was she doing? What if Thomas ever found out? It would kill him, it will ruin their lives. It would be the end of them. She had no choice, she decided. She had to let go ...

The hands made their way slowly down the insides of her legs. This time just brushing her thighs with the gloves and traveling down her shins to her feet. She had never had anyone touch her feet in a sexual way before. Gloves brushed first the tops and then the bottoms of both feet. Slowly, slowly causing her legs to tighten.

He moved up her body to her breasts. He cupped each breast and pinched the nipples, playing with her feelings of deep desire as if he wanted her to beg through her bindings and gag.

He was alternating his left hand between her nipples while his right hand moved down again slowly. He let it drag over her tummy, past her navel and began circling his fingers around her vagina.

He changed his pattern and lifted his hands. He placed each hand on the side of her upper body and dragged them down as if outlining her curves on the bed. He continued down her hips, thighs and calves. Right down to her heels. Then he reached between her legs and repeated the exercise, outlining the insides of her legs.

He started to rub her feet again, massaging the arches and toes. Her thighs felt rigid and her ass tightened up. Hard, tight lower body, but her upper body was still relaxed. Until suddenly he stopped rubbing her feet and grasped both her breasts in his gloved hands, while working her nipples between his fingers. She tried to cry out again, behind her gag.

Oh my God, she thought. I can't resist.

He touched her clit again and she exploded for the second time. Feelings of intense pleasure and release, her mind saw vivid colors of heaven.

She was kissed very lightly on the lips as she drifted off with the ultimate pleasures washing over her entire body.

chapter ten

She awoke with the ring around her left middle finger. She pulled and released herself. She quickly gathered everything from the bed and tucked it away in her drawer.

How did he find everything in my drawer? she wondered. He must have spent some time nosing around. When?

She looked at herself in the mirror before her shower. Pen marks and lines were over her stomach, her breasts, her legs and her lower belly. She ran her fingers down a couple of the lines and smiled. The memories came alive, that incredible feeling flooded her brain. The feeling of total euphoria while under his control.

What am I going to do? Do I keep this secret or try to catch the bastard? I am a Chicago Police detective. I should be trying to catch the guy. He can't get away with this. He's invading my privacy, stripping me down to nothing and practically doing anything he wants to me. Anything I want him to do to me? He's a monster isn't he?

It was wrong and she knew it. But it just felt so good. Damn it. She was strong. She could get through this. She was a cop and cops don't give up and beg for help. She couldn't let it get out … for Thomas's and her parents' sake. She remembered how both her mom and her dad were so disappointed when she told them she was going to become a cop. They had thought she should proceed with a more feminine career, like being a nurse or a teacher.

Fuck that, she wanted to kill the bastard. And she had the gun to do it. Sometimes life didn't always seem fair.

Like the lady they recently caught who kept breaking into houses, cleaning them and then leaving her bill to be paid by the home owner. Who was harmed? But the house was still broken into so someone had to pay. It was the cleaner who paid in the end, jail time and a fine.

Sam showered and dressed for work. She grabbed her gun from the safe in the bottom drawer and shoved it home into its holster. She used a shoulder holster under her leather jacket just like her male counterparts. She liked the feel of the gun under her arm. She could feel it almost always when she moved and she liked that. When she used to keep it on her waist, she found it was too bulky and interfered with any sweater or jacket she wanted to wear.

She looked at herself in the mirror. She smiled. She thought she looked relaxed. She left the house and hit the freeway.

A half hour or so later she was having a hard time concentrating on the case. Robert was telling her about the latest break in the Anderson case. They had found that the husband Marshal was off the hook. Turned out he was out of town in Los Angeles the night of the murder.

Almost nothing new had been discovered for two weeks and then suddenly bang, a new lead. Robert had finally got evidence against the lover, Barry Cummings. Witnesses could place he and Connie Anderson together. They figured the couple were actually banging each other every chance they got. The shower, the car, the super market, the local church.

Sam and Robert were standing by the long counter at the back of the squad room which held the old coffee machine. Normally the room smelled a little of sweat mixed with dust and piss and blood, but today all Sam could smell was cologne.

"Can you believe it," joked Robert as he poured himself a coffee, "the fucking church! They were meeting whenever they could and doing the big jiggle in a fucking church. Amazing. Hey partner, what's the matter?"

"Nothing," Sam replied. "Just tired I guess."

"All those late nights with hubby eh? How's Thomas doing?"

"Good I guess, he's in Washington for the next few days," she replied.

"Again?" Robert looked surprised. "Oh I get it, you guys are trying to work it out huh?"

"No!" Samantha was shocked. "It's not like that at all. He's just been really busy lately and away on a lot of trips. We aren't having any problems Robert." Maybe she sounded a little too defensive.

Sam walked to her desk and sat. She frowned. They weren't having any problems were they? She thought they always got along. It was true, he was away a lot lately, but he said it would only be for another few months. In the spring he said his position was going to be changing where he would be home in Chicago most of the time.

"So here's what we got." Robert said. "As you can see, it looks as if Barry got mad when Connie tried to break off their affair. We got him on tape threatening her, he sounded really pissed."

"You think? Doesn't make him a murderer though," Sam said slowly. She was still thinking of Thomas. What was he doing away? Could he be having an affair? Could he be seeing someone else? Maybe he was leading a double life? With Sam for a week here or there and a week or two with another woman. Another family. Fuck.

Are you keeping secrets from me Thomas? How do I ask him? Are you really leading a double life? Her thoughts startled her and she froze searching for an answer. Oh fuck.

"You ok?" Robert asked. "You look a little shaken."

Sam shook her head and waved him off.

"Well whatever," Robert said, "he threatened her and we have to talk to the bastard. But first we have to find him. Now if he's going underground, where would he go?"

chapter eleven

Sam's week didn't exactly go as planned. First off Tuesday morning her car wouldn't start and she had to phone Robert to come and pick her up for work. The car had to be towed. Turned out to be a faulty alternator, but it took two days to get it back on the road.

Next, Tuesday afternoon a water main on her street blew up and the entire block had to be closed for most of the week. She didn't have running water in her house for three days so she was stopping by Natalie's apartment each morning to shower.

And lastly, a robbery took place across the street and down a block from their house Thursday night which involved two deaths. A drive by shooting at a small pizza joint killing two gang members is what Sam had heard at work. NAGIS, The Narcotics and Gang Investigation Section were in charge of the investigation, but Sam had offered to help out if they needed any information about the area. It turned out though, the two victims weren't even from Chicago so her local knowledge wasn't really very helpful.

"God it's a good thing you weren't out getting a pizza on Thursday," Thomas said. He was talking to Sam on the phone from Washington.

Sam was sitting at the kitchen table Saturday afternoon. Sunlight was trying to break through the clouds, but losing out to rain. Only grey poured through every window. A cup of hot coffee sat on the table in front of her. Her gun and handcuffs sat in the drawer in the living room. She was dressed for the gym and was on her way out the door when Thomas had called.

"Yah they tell me there were at least three shooters," Sam said, "and they sprayed the place up pretty good too … it's a wonder that more bodies weren't piled up."

"Hasn't happened for a while around our area has it," he said, "guess it was bound to happen again eventually."

"So tell me how is Washington?"

"Alright I guess," he said, "I'll be home tomorrow night. I miss you."

Sam wondered if that was true. He sounded genuine. "I miss you too ..."

She sat and pondered. She wondered where Thomas really was and who he could be with. She wondered if she knew the other woman. She wondered if the other woman even knew that Sam existed. She wondered if it was too late or if anything could be worked out. She knew she had to talk to Thomas about many things but she wanted to do it in person, not over the phone.

She no longer felt like working out so she decided to go to the gun range instead. She kind of felt like shooting something or someone, she just wasn't sure who. She pulled her Glock from the drawer and walked quickly out the front door and into the rain to find her car.

She drove to her favourite indoor range, a private place tucked away near the center of the city, called Donnie's Indoor Range. But when she pulled up at Donnie's, her cell phone rang. She parked and answered it. It was Thomas again.

"Hey darling," he said, "I forgot to tell you … I may have to go to Europe for a while."

"When?" Sam asked.

"Not sure but I don't think it will be for a month at least."

"For how long?"

"Probably no more than two or three months," he said.

"Where are you going?"

"Not sure. We haven't figured out an itinerary yet ... but I just thought I would let you know before I forgot."

"Well thanks for ruining my weekend Thomas," Sam said as she broke the connection.

She sat back in the seat and thought about what Thomas had just said. If he really was going to Europe for a while she should be able to track his location fairly easily this time, just so she could feel satisfied that he wasn't lying to her.

He couldn't be leading a double life, could he? Could I just come out and ask him, she wondered. Should I ask him? Corner him?

She sat and watched the rain drops accumulate on the windshield. The window seemed like her life lately. It had all started out clear a few weeks ago, she was happy, had nothing to hide, was content, or at least that's what she kept telling herself. But lately, since someone had decided to turn her life upside down, her life was now fast becoming clouded-over, muddy, murky, colors and reflections bouncing in all directions, unable to make any connection to anything remotely like a normal life.

She suddenly felt detached. She wondered where her life was going. Where her marriage was going. She stared at the windshield. Tears began to roll down her cheeks as if being absorbed through the windows. She felt so alone.

Sam sat for many minutes just watching and listening to the rain. Finally, she shook away her sorrow and decided she still felt like shooting something or someone. She entered Donnie's and found the place empty. Donnie was slumped behind the front counter, reading some sort of trade magazine.

"Hey Donnie," Sam tried to sound chipper.

"Yah," Donnie said, "you want jacket or hollow points?"

"Full metals." Sam had known Donnie for years now and had probably said two or three words to him ever. He was as friendly as a brick and Sam figured he probably had the personality of one as well.

As she stood loading and preparing her Glock, she turned and looked at Donnie again. She felt ill watching him read. She was thirty feet away but could still smell him. He obviously never used cologne and she actually figured he never even showered very regularly either. He weighed at least 300 pounds and seemed to always wear the same clothes. Oh God ... She didn't even want to think about it.

Sam turned back quickly, dragged the headphones over her head with her left hand, raised her pistol and took aim. She let off three quick rounds before hesitating. Three to the head of target at the other end of the range. That was one of the reasons she liked Donnie's so much, the targets. Accurate distances and plain, easy to see entire human shaped targets. Great for her training. Shadows of men just waiting to get ripped apart by her Glock.

She knew she shouldn't be at the range when she was so angry. She let off another three rounds. There was no getting around it, the shooting seemed to be great therapy.

She thought of Connie's death and let off a couple more quick rounds. Her shooting seemed a bit off but she didn't care, it just felt good.

She thought of Thomas and all the times he was away lately. She let off three more shots. And she thought of him going to be away for a few months. She emptied the clip and reloaded.

She changed targets and emptied another clip. She noticed Donnie's reflection in the glass partition. He was staring at her as if he thought she was nuts. She didn't care, she reloaded and emptied it again.

Then she thought of her mysterious lover. Her secret manipulator. Her real life fantasy. She aimed and let one shot go right between the eyes.

chapter twelve

She lay still in the dark.

He was close, but she relaxed.

He was circling her lower belly with his gloves again. Slowly getting closer to her clit. The waves of tension started to build again. She decided to let it build without conflict.

She let the gloves charge her body with their touch. She felt relaxed and accepting.

She felt a mouth slowly close around her right nipple as he leaned over her body. His weight pressed down on her stomach. For some reason she felt completely helpless and captive, but very safe and secure. He was hiding her. Protecting her from the world.

He sucked repeatedly, hard then soft. He switched to her left nipple. Again hard then soft. She could barely breath. She had to concentrate to breath. And she was wet.

He slid his hands down between her legs and pulled her lips apart very slowly and deliberately. His gloved fingers didn't probe, they didn't enter. He had other things in mind.

Her mind was exploding with desire. She felt herself get very wet. Wet and in need.

She tried to arch her back and cry out but was held down again by her secure bindings and silenced by the gag. Her breathing went shallow. Her mind raced. Oh my God, she thought.

And then the gloves stopped. She gasped as he lifted off the bed.

"No ..." she tried to say through the gag. But all was quiet.

She waited.

Suddenly she heard a loud slurp and she felt a slight pain between her breasts. No not pain ... cold. An ice cube was being moved around her body. It touched her nipples, shocking Sam with the cold electric touch. Her body stiffened as her mind felt like screaming. Every cell in her skin reacted as if currents were running through her. She held her breath.

The ice cube was rubbed slowly around each nipple creating the most amazing feeling. Oh fuck, she screamed inside. I have never felt anything like this before, she thought.

The ice disappeared as he massaged water into her breasts like lotion. She heard him take another ice cube from a glass and with a slurp pull it from his mouth. He dropped the cold cube onto her belly and slid it around her navel.

"Ah," was all she could get out through her gag, holy fuck was what she was thinking inside. What an incredible feeling. Something she had never experienced before. He started down her lower belly with the ice and between her legs. He pulled her vagina lips apart again. Sam gasped at the touch.

My God, she thought, he is so close and I am so wet. This is so bad so why does it feel so good?

He slowly pushed the ice cube inside her. It felt so good going in but the feeling soon ended and she was holding the water in. He opened her again and the cold water leaked out onto the bed.

He pinched her nipples lightly again. Harder, she thought, I can take it. Please. Please. I am so wet and horny. Am I asking for him again? Oh my god, I can't take this. I need him inside, but, but ...

He started down her belly with his mouth. Oh my fuck, she felt everything building. I can't believe this, she thought. She felt slightly light-headed and dizzy as he moved down to her clit and motioned his tongue in circles around her magic spot. First wide circles, then narrow.

He continued holding her lips open as he ran his tongue hard around her vagina.

Her nerves were screaming inside. Yes, yes, yes, she thought.

His tongue moved closer and closer to her clit. It seemed like ages when it finally found her most vulnerable spot and he started to flick back and forth. The feeling was so incredible, she exploded suddenly. She just exploded, inside and out. She came in one long and hard orgasm as he continued to lick around her clit and lips lightly. As she started to relax and breath again, he started to enter her with his tongue. He pulled her lips apart and sunk his tongue deep inside her. She felt every nerve ending in her vagina jump as he pulled his tongue out slowly and sunk it back in.

He reached up and brushed her nipples with his gloved hands. He brushed around her breasts and down to her navel as his tongue continued its job of probing deeper and deeper inside her. She had never had this kind of attention paid to her vagina before. She couldn't believe how it was igniting her sexuality. A real feeling of intimacy began to build inside, a strange bond between her and her captor. She felt his teachings were opening up a world of pleasure that she didn't even know existed. She wanted more.

He let her catch her breath for a moment while he moved up and sucked on first her left nipple and then her right. He brushed his hand down between her legs and felt her wetness. She waited, she wanted him inside. She wanted to plead but it was useless against the gag.

He moved down to her navel and circled it twice with his tongue. Then he moved lower.

Her body gave out and exploded a second time when he tongued her clit lightly back and forth. She felt her brain twist open in mindless pleasure. Her feelings of extreme sensitivity shot waves of electricity through every nerve in her tightly wound body.

She was exhausted. Her mind went blank and she fell into a light sleep.

She awoke. How long? she wondered.

She untied herself and put everything away. She showered and dressed in a dark navy skirt and light blue blouse she hadn't worn in ages. It was one of Thomas's favorites he always said. She had the day off and she decided to go shopping.

She had more spring in her step walking between the racks at Saks. As she passed other woman, she smiled and thought to herself how good she felt. Alive and free.

And wholly satisfied. Her body felt rested but somehow glowing at the same time. She hadn't felt this good for a long time.

She sat outside at Duffie's Cafe for lunch and ordered a clubhouse. She relaxed and thought about her mysterious lover. The hands with such intimate knowledge of her. He knew all what she wanted and craved. It wasn't as though she had missed these feelings before. She didn't even know she could miss them. She had never experienced anything like this hunger, this deep craving in her core.

She started to feel hot and realized she could easily become moist if she thought anymore about her lover. She flushed ... she felt her face must be red with embarrassment. She looked around the restaurant and wondered if anyone could guess what she was thinking.

The waiter? The bartender? Could they see on her face what deep and dark thoughts were running through her head? What dirty and nasty things she imagined, were being planned by her secret lover?

She felt like she just wanted to disappear off of the planet. She remembered back when she was really young, maybe eleven or twelve years old ... the first time she recognized her own sexual feelings ... her

awkwardness … her embarrassment. Sam
and her parents were over at a relative's
house at Christmas … the kids in the
basement … they were playing a game.
Hide and seek or murder or something.
She was hiding behind the freezer, sitting
crunched up in a ball with her knees
tucked up to her chin. As she hid in the
dark, she became aware of her urge to
touch herself between her legs. For the
first time she wanted to rub herself and
felt naughty at the thought … she couldn't
help herself … she reached out and found
a pillow laying by her hiding spot.

She folded the pillow over and shoved it
between her legs grabbing it with her
thighs pulling it up and into herself. She
felt so confused and yet so warm and safe.
She was hiding for what seemed like hours
but was probably only minutes. Without
warning … the light clicked on … all the
cousins, almost all at once, were suddenly
standing around her laughing and pointing
… the pillow had been covered in rust and
oil. It was all over her crotch … her three
older cousins were laughing the hardest …
she flushed with shame … embarrassed
beyond belief, she had just wished that she
could have disappeared off the planet. Instead, she had run upstairs to her mother.

They had tried to rub it out of her jeans but instead had made it worse. And for the rest of the meal she had to sit with rust and oil smeared all down her crotch.

Sam shook herself out of her memories. Could anyone in this world really guess that right now she could actually rip off all of her clothes and run around the streets naked? If only people could read other people's thoughts ... she wondered ... oh my God ... The world would really be a fucked up place.

She flushed again at her own secret thoughts, the guilt rose up in her. What is happening to me? She thought. What has this new secret life done to me? I am becoming a perverted mess and I can't even let anyone know what is happening. Holy fuck, I don't want anyone to know!

chapter thirteen

Loud Bells, confusion! Chaos!

Fucking alarm clock. Fucking Thursday mornings. Way too early.

Thomas had come home Late Sunday night and then left again Tuesday morning for New York. Sam didn't really get much of a chance to talk with him Monday night. She was starting to feel like her world was being torn apart. Absent husband who may or may not be living a double life, stranger who was playing her body like a harp and fucking with her mind like cheap drugs. And now the unsolvable murder of a woman who seemed to be living a completely normal life. Normal except she also seemed to have a secret lover, just like Sam.

The office seemed quiet that morning. Most of the force must be out on the street, Sam thought. She and Robert sat in the main boardroom looking through files stacked on the table.

"Okay," Robert said. "You've only got a couple of hundred bucks to your name and you're hiding out. Plus most of us are out on the street looking for you … where would you hide? He hasn't run, we've covered the airports, trains, buses, you name it. We've tried all the hotels and motels, right down to trailer parks. God it seems like we've been looking for this guy forever, but it's only been just over a week so far."

"Let me see those top files will you," Sam said snapping her fingers. "I just got an idea."

"Huh," said Robert.

"Look at his job list for this month. See the ones that haven't been completed, like this one," she said pointing to the list. "Most homeowners are still around in their house while he's doing their work. But look at this, a couple have moved out temporarily to a hotel while the work is being done to their house."

"Yah there's two on the list," Robert said.

"I'll bet you he's squatting in the most remote one," Sam said.

"Smart girl," Robert was smiling at Sam.

"Hey that's why they pay me the big bucks," Sam replied.

"This one," Robert said pointing near the bottom of the list. "Let's go!"

chapter fourteen

Sam and Robert were back. The successful capture of Barry Cummings had both partners in a good mood. Sure enough they had found Barry hiding out in the fairly remote home past Oak Park.

"I didn't kill Connie!" Barry was pleading. "I loved her."

"Then why were you hiding out Barry, innocent people don't run," Robert said jabbing his finger at Barry.

"I wasn't hiding, I was working …" Barry leaned back and threw up his hands, "I was just staying over while I was renovating their entire main level."

"Then why didn't you even tell your answering service where you were," Sam said leaning forward, "you were hiding from us Barry, we know it … you know it … and you know we know it."

"Okay, okay, you got me, I was hiding out. But only because I knew you guys would be pinning me to the murder. And I didn't do it!"

"Oh yah Barry," Robert said, "If you didn't kill her, then prove it to us. Where were you on the night of the twenty forth?"

"I was visiting my mother," Barry said. "She's in a nursing home in Kenosha."

"We'll need the name of that home Barry," Sam said. "And your alibi better be solid or you're going down big time."

Sam stood and motioned for Robert to follow her.

Barry was left sitting in Interrogation room three when Robert followed Sam out into the hallway.

"So what do you think?" Sam asked, "do you believe him?"

"Well I don't know but we don't have any other suspects right now." answered Robert.

"That means …" Sam froze. She could actually feel the blood drain from her face. She turned away not wanting Robert to notice.

"Yup," said Robert, "maybe a complete stranger broke in and tortured and killed her. Or maybe someone was stalking her or maybe she had another secret lover, some-one other than Barry. Maybe we have to start thinking like it's some crazy psycho-pathic freak, I'll start checking for any pat-terns, you know similar MO's around the area."

Oh God, thought Sam. She was already walking fast down the hall.

She slipped into the upper floor wash-room and into stall number two. The stall with the sign marked Private hanging on it. All the ladies in the Precinct had agreed years ago to allow quiet time to take place in stall two, think time, no one used it for the obvious purpose. Of course you could use it to go pee when you had to, but absolutely no number two's. There was even some graffiti scrawled across one wall that read "Number Two - no Number twos!" And "Sitting but no Shitting!"

Sam reached down and placed the piece of wood on top of the seat. The ladies had also agreed that they would keep a piece of plywood leaning against the back of the stall. It was to be used as a seat for your clothes when you needed it.

She sat down in a daze. Her eyes were flooded with tears.

Holy fuck, she thought. What if the person who kept snatching her was a stranger, a killer, a deranged psychopath? What if next time she was the one with the belt around her neck and the pantyhose shoved down her throat?

She was silent. She sat still. She was sure there was no blood left in her head. She felt dizzy and in shock.

There was a stranger loose in her neighborhood and he was raping her? Wasn't he? Wasn't he? Oh fuck, she thought. It can't be. Can it?

Her mysterious lover had soft hands, a soft touch, wonderful tongue. Not the tongue of a psychopath, she was sure of that. It can't be.

"Fuck," she said out loud. "Fuck, fuck, fuck!"

I have to find out, she thought. I have to know who it is. This cannot go on without knowing who it is.

She sat still, her mascara streaking as tears rolled down her cheeks and puddled on the floor.

chapter fifteen

Sam needed help. She knew there was only one person she wanted to get to help - one of her closest friends, Alex, from the Crime Lab. Sam cleaned herself up, slipped out the back and drove over to the lab.

Alexis Sheffield was a tall beautiful redhead. She was always seen in her black, large-rimmed glasses and business suits under her lab coat. Her dark red hair was usually pinned back in a ponytail but today was loosely spilling over her shoulders.

"Alex," Sam said. "Have you got a minute?" Alex was in the lab, bent over her microscope.

"Of course Sam," she answered not looking up. "Just a sec."

A moment later she straightened up and turned to look at Sam.

"Oh my God," Alex said, "you look terrible. Are you okay Sam?" Alex hugged Sam and held her close.

Sam began to melt. She felt no support from her legs. She could only feel Alex holding her up. Slowly Sam began to cry.

Standing in the lab holding onto Alex tightly, Sam didn't care if anyone else was witnessing her breakdown. She just kept crying. Alex kept holding.

They slowly moved toward a stool and Alex forced Sam to sit.

"Baby," said Alex bending over Sam and wiping her tears away with a tissue, "you have to tell me what's wrong. Is it Thomas?"

"No, no," Sam said between sobs. "It's nothing like that. It isn't Thomas … its when he goes away …"

"What?"

And she began to tell Alex everything. From a few Sundays ago when she was snatched for the first time up to her latest discovery. When her and Robert had just put two and two together and realized it might have been a deranged psychopath who had last been with Connie, instead of their suspect, Barry.

Could this be a random act or the actions of someone who was following Sam, stalking her, toying with her for weeks as her secret lover? Sam and Alex wondered. Could the same guy that killed Connie now be toying with Sam?

Sam had been denying her own common sense. Up until now she hadn't been all that concerned about her secret lover, it just felt so incredibly good. But now it had turned serious. She realized it was no longer a game.

Sam felt incredibly tired and overwhelmed when she had finished telling Alex everything. She slumped down and put her head in her hands while Alex sat staring at her.

"Holy shit," was all Alex could say.

"You see," Sam said sitting up, "I need to find out who it is. Who's the asshole seducing me when my husband goes away. He may have been stalking me for a long time and knows when Thomas leaves the house."

"Wow that is just fucking scary!" said Alex.

"Well ... I know it's hard to believe, but somehow so far I've felt quite safe while he's playing with me. It's as if he is trying to make me enjoy the pleasure of it all. But oh my God is it the pleasure before something? Is he preparing me for something? Before he tires of me and I end up like Connie."

"Oh my God," Alex said, "do you really think it's the same guy?"

"No idea," Sam said, "but if it is, I have to catch him and catch him quickly, before he hurts me or anyone else again."

"Well you have to tell Thomas!" Alex said.

"Definitely not! I can't tell anyone - no one can know - you have to promise me you won't tell anyone," pleaded Sam. "Especially not Thomas ... especially not him. He'd kill me. What could I ever tell Thomas anyway, your wife is being ravished by a stranger right in your own bed! I don't think so."

"Fucking weird all right," Alex said. "We have to come up with a way to figure out who it is or how you can catch him."

"And I can't figure out what it is that he is using to knock me out each time," said Sam.

"We'll have to work on that as well then," said Alex. "Let me think about it. Go home and get some rest, you look exhausted. Or do you think it's safe? Maybe you should stay at my place tonight?"

"I'll be fine Alex," Sam said, "but thanks for the help ... I really appreciate it ... I think I just need some sleep."

"We'll talk tomorrow," Alex said, "over lunch, my treat."

chapter sixteen

Sam held the door open and followed Alex into the food court. Considering all the junk food she had consumed lately, Sam thought it was a good thing that Alex had suggested something a little more healthy. She and Alex both got in line at Main's Home-Style Cafe.

Sam picked the egg salad on whole wheat, Alex had a split grape and radish salad. At least Sam didn't have to feel guilty about what she was going to be shoveling down her throat for once. Most meals nowadays it seemed, were greasy burgers and fries from O'Malley's down the street. But today she wanted to eat light. To feel clean and healthy. She had gone home and crashed on the couch last night and slept straight through. She awoke refreshed. A little stiff, but refreshed.

Alex sat down with her back to the bright window. The glow from the sun surrounded her head and back. Samantha placed her tray opposite Alex and sat looking at her friend. My God, she thought, Alex is so beautiful with her long flowing and loosely curled red hair. Her flawless skin and face and her bright green eyes dancing around behind her cute glasses.

"So what's new?" Sam asked.

"Got a lead on a new 15 Mantle," Alex said.

"Huh," Sam looked confused.

"Sorry I mean a 51 Mantle. 1951. Mickey Mantle. Going to look after work today."

Sam laughed as she thought about Alex and her funny habit of collecting baseball cards. She was always going through dusty old garage sales hunting for any illusive cards – something she could claim as a fortune.

"Wow, well good luck with that," Sam said. "Might help if you didn't keep mixing up the dates."

"Yah well, it's just me and my numbers thing," Alex smiled, "I sometimes reverse them in my head."

"I just wondered if you've had a chance to think through my problem?" Sam took a bite of her sandwich. Not enough mayo she thought.

"Yup, got it," Alex said. "You already told me fingerprints are out, the bastard wears gloves ... so here's what we're going to do. First off, you'll have to get me a sample of the bastard's fluid from something like his semen ... saliva ... whatever. Or even get me a fingernail or hair."

She took a sip of coffee and continued.

"Then you can go around and collect samples from all the guys you suspect in your life until we find a match ... then you can kill the bastard."

"Hey I told you it wasn't like that," Sam blurted. She hesitated. "He is so kind and gentle ... and so hot ... his hands are ..."

"Whatever. Anyone who thinks they should be doing that is seriously fucked up if you ask me."

"It's just different that's all." What the hell was she thinking, of course it was fucked up, so fucked up. And yet she almost felt dizzy when she thought back to her bedroom ... and his touch.

"We'll nail the bastard. Just wait."

"So how are we supposed to run his DNA anyway?" Sam asked. "I thought the tests were covered and all tracked by the department?"

"Don't worry about that," Alex said, "I can get around that. And I'll be doing most of it late at night so no one will know. The only thing we have to worry about is MacKetchison's prying eyes."

"Thanks Alex," Sam said as she placed her hand onto Alex's. "I really appreciate it."

"Ah … no problem Sam, there is no way we are going to let this bastard get away with this. We'll string him up by his balls and skin him alive."

"What a visual Alex … and I'm still eating."

"So you may have to get a little creative next time, if there is a next time … to get his sample," Alex said.

"What do you mean?" Sam asked.

"Well how about saliva, you know when he licked you? Was there any, you know, extra saliva that you could swab for me?"

"No," Sam said, "not really."

"The ice? Na that's no good. It would have all melted. How about any of the bindings?"

"Not really," Sam repeated.

"Got it!" Alex snapped her fingers, "leave a glass of wine out by your bed. Wait - skip the wine, it's always late morning or early afternoon right … Thomas will suspect something. Just put a cold glass of water by your bed. The bastard will take a sip, guaranteed, and most people don't realize we can actually pull a sample from where their lips and cheeks touch the glass. It's not that easy but I can do it."

"Okay," Sam said, "that'll work. Now what about the stuff he is using to knock me out?"

"Right," Alex answered. "I forgot about that ... I'll see what I can do, maybe there will be trace left on you that I can swab and analyze. Call me right after the next session and I'll come over and check, okay?"

"I guess," Sam said slowly, thinking how uncomfortable that encounter would be. To have Alex walk in swabbing everything in sight right after another encounter.

"How about I just swab my mouth or maybe the gag he used and we can see from there?"

"Yah, that'll probably work," said Alex, "I just need a couple of good wipes."

"I'll see what I can do."

"Hey are you going to finish that?" Alex asked pointing to Sam's pickle.

"No, help yourself." Sam smiled.

chapter seventeen

Sam lay on her bed worried that her life was falling apart. It seemed as though she had no recollection of what her life was like before all this stress. She couldn't remember the last time her and Thomas had made love. Was it Valentine's day? Or was it back in January?

She felt as though everything had gotten out of control. What could she do? She wondered where Thomas was and what he was doing. He wouldn't be back for three more days.

Her worry gave way to other feelings. Confusion and love and neglect and the truth all swirled around in her head.

The bedroom matched. Messy, her clothes laying around the floor. Thomas would usually be the one to pick up after her, he was way more tidy. But even he had learned to live with the mess in their house. In fact the only room that could be considered finished was the kitchen. The rest of the house had construction written all over it, smelling of sawdust and paint.

She lay naked on the bed after just stepping out of the shower. She hadn't dried herself. She reached down between her legs and rubbed her wet body. Oh Christ she thought, I am so in need of those hands again. The crashing orgasms coming from them, the desire to be handled again. Her left hand began to rub her vagina up and down as her right hand reached up and began playing first with one nipple, then the other.

She thought of Thomas and his body and his penis. How she longed to stroke him, it had been way too long. She wanted him inside of her. Oh Thomas, she thought, what am I going to do?

Suddenly without reason she felt guilty. Her hands stopped and she pulled a sheet over herself for cover.

Covering up sparked a memory. She remembered back when she was fifteen ... at her best friends house. At the time she had a boyfriend named Blayne. They had been dating for a few months. He was a kind and polite boy who was normally fairly quiet. He was tall and skinny with long brown hair. He liked sports and reading she remembered. He and Sam seemed to have the same sense of humor and she got along with Blayne better than any other boy she knew at the time. But one night Blayne was out playing football with the team and three of them were sitting around while everyone else was out for the night ... or so it seemed ... Sue and Samantha had been hanging around the mall most of the evening when they met up with this cute sixteen year old named Ronnie from school.

They had brought him back to Sue's house because Samantha thought Sue really liked him and maybe was hoping to make out with him or something. Sue's house was a massive two story Victorian style house with a large games room on the main floor.

They had been sitting around watching television when suddenly out of the blue, Sue suggested a game of strip pool. Well of course Ronnie jumped at the chance to play with the two girls but Samantha wanted to go home. Sue had pulled her aside and convinced her to play ... that it would be a real laugh ... that it was no harm ... just a bit of fun ... and that Ronnie had never played pool on her dad's full-sized snooker table before so he would probably suck anyway.

The game got underway and of course Samantha started loosing badly. The other two had only lost one article of clothing each while Sam was down to just her bra and panties and one sock left. Sue had gone upstairs to get another drink when suddenly the basement was full of football players. Their football game had ended and they had all piled into the back of Sue's brother's pick up truck and driven straight home.

She shook with embarrassment while grabbing her clothes and trying to put them on. Nervously trying to explain to Blayne that nothing was going on, but he wouldn't believe her. She begged and pleaded with him to understand that it was Sue who had started the game, and she had just left the room. But he could only believe what he saw, he kept repeating. It looked to him like they were about to go at it. He was crushed, he said. He had really liked Sam and thought they really hit it off. He felt totally betrayed. She felt so much guilt then, when he said that. How could she have been so stupid?

She felt bad about that night for months after. She would cry in bed most nights from guilt. And her reputation at school was never the same. Blayne left her that night and she was never alone with him again. And she had really like Blayne …

What can I do Thomas? she said to herself. I know I am cheating on you but it's not my fault. It is not my fault! Is it?

chapter eighteen

Sam sat at her precinct desk and started writing out a list of every male she knew. She decided it was a male that was her secret lover, couldn't be a female. No female would be able to subdue her that easily. And it had to be someone that knew her … in fact someone that knew her fairly well at least.

She started her list with the suspect Barry Cummings. Next came her partner Robert and then all of her other colleagues from work. She then went right through other acquaintances and then her personal friends.

There were twenty nine males on the list. She then went down the list and crossed off all the guys who were either married, gay or out of town.

She was left with a list of eleven. Eleven potential suspects. One of the eleven must be her secret lover, her secret orgasmic controller, her secret heaven.

And she had to find out who it was.

Sam didn't need to worry about collecting the DNA from Barry Cummings, it was already on file. They had collected it the moment he became a prime suspect in

Connie's murder. She checked off the first name.

Next on her list, Robert. She leaned back in her chair and thought about her partner, Robert Shore. Although he was only in his mid forties, his dark hair was brushed back and just beginning to grey at the temples. It made Robert look very distinguished, very handsome and worldly looking. He had the look of an aging movie star.

She started to feel uncomfortable and restless when she sat there dreaming that they could be Robert's hands that were caressing her body and entering her most private areas.

She stood to go for a walk. Get out and think, get away from the stuffy room. She took the back stairs up to the roof. Looking out across the water, she thought back to the days when her secret lover had played with her body. Orchestrating her feelings into one orgasm after another, seemed like it was all perfectly timed. Where each day, her pleasure built up from moment to moment, where she had no control but didn't care. Did she? She could just lay back and enjoy each feeling without worrying … couldn't she? But it still just didn't seem right.

She thought about Robert. How could her partner of nine years ever do something like this? It wasn't so much that she thought of Robert as a father figure, but more of an older brother, knowing so much about each other. She was so comfortable with Robert. She shivered at the thoughts of Robert's hands circling her crotch.

She remembered back to when she was fifteen in the summer at the cabin with Sue and Sue's parents. A friend of Sue's dad had offered to drive her into town to meet up with Sue and her mother who had left a couple of hours before. Sue's dad was fixing the boat so he couldn't go. Samantha had agreed to go with the guy, she couldn't even remember his name, but remembered he was really cute. Long blond hair, looked like a surfer. He had an Australian accent. She had a bit of a crush. But of course she remembered he was at least twice her age.

At the time she had felt a twang of pride that she was getting to ride in this guys truck alone. Just him and Sam. He was so cute and he was so interesting, always talking about his life. She was in awe. She felt so privileged. So grown up.

Samantha was wearing just her bikini at the time she agreed to go but decided to throw on her shorts and a halter top just before jumping into the truck. He noticed her clothes and mentioned how much he liked the cut and color of her bathing suit.

Half way to town surfer dude pretended to have trouble with the truck. Sam couldn't remember if the truck really did have a problem or not, but in any case, it stopped in the middle of nowhere. He turned to her and said something about having to wait for someone to come along, maybe they should take a walk in the woods. At the time she froze and just wanted out. Tears had started to run down her cheeks when he reached over to her thighs and started brushing her shorts. She was so scared, she didn't dare move. She had sat quietly while he had caressed both her breasts under her top and bathing suit. Tears started down her face. He had reached into her shorts and was rubbing her clit hard. He tried to enter her with his middle finger but was unable to really get anywhere because of the angle of his hand and her tight shorts. She had closed her eyes and refused to look. Tears still streamed down both cheeks. He suddenly withdrew his hand as Sue and her mother drove up. But he still managed to secretly smile at Sam as he sniffed his fingers.

She never told anyone that summer of the encounter. Even when she had to be around surfer dude for the rest of the summer. In fact, she never spoke of it to anyone.

How can you not trust a good friend of your best friend's father? Sam thought. The asshole. What the fuck had she ever done to him that made him decide he had the right to do anything to her body? Who did he think he was? Fucking Asshole … she shuddered at the memory of his hands on her that summer.

She watched the reflections dancing off the water as her mind came back into focus. She turned and walked down the back stairs with the only thought that it can't be Robert. It just can't be.

She entered the Homicide room and approached her desk. Sam and Robert both had the type of desks that you see in old banks and schoolrooms, light varnished wood with sticky drawers and broken handles.

She looked around the squad room but no one was paying any attention to her. She sat at Robert's desk and started to look around for something with his DNA on it.

"Hey partner," Robert surprised her, "can I help you with something?"

"Sorry," Sam said a little too quickly after being startled. "I was just looking for your notes on Cummings. Are we still holding him?"

"Nope, he was released last night, around 8:00pm. After Davis checked his alibi he told me he let him go. It all checked out."

"Damn," Sam let out. "I just wanted to ask him something."

"Here's my notes on the interview," Robert said as he pulled the papers from his briefcase.

Sam returned to her desk and pretended to look through the papers as if she was really looking for something.

The phone rang. Robert reached for it before Sam moved.

"Detective Shore," Robert said into the phone. "Shit, your kidding … okay … we'll be there right away."

He hung up and reached for his coat.

"Let's go partner," he said to Sam. "There's been another murder."

chapter nineteen

Sam looked around the bedroom very slowly and carefully. The maid had found Angela Cooper tied naked and kneeling by the bed facing it. Hands tied behind her back with a bathrobe belt, another regular belt tightly around her neck. Open mouth gag holding her mouth open with a pair of pantyhose stuffed down her throat. Her eyes hidden behind a leather mask.

Same MO, Sam thought. Although she hadn't seen the original crime scene of Connie, she had looked over the photos many times and knew the scene well. Things here looked the same.

To Sam it looked as though the bed hadn't been slept in last night. Even though the bed wasn't made, the covers had been thrown on loosely as if someone had made a half hearted attempt. But there were some indentations in the bedding near the body. Someone had been sitting on the bed right in front of poor Angela, probably while they were killing her, thought Sam.

Poor Angela. She looked so helpless tied up by the bed. Probably kneeling in front of her captor, begging for her life. Sam tried not to tear up but it was difficult. She had to keep wiping her eyes.

Cut it out, Sam thought. Your a cop! And cops aren't supposed to cry. Idiot.

To distract herself, she slowly walked around the room examining the edges of the crime scene. Robert was over talking with one of the Medical Examiners and the forensic technician about the body.

On the walls were prints of famous paintings, a Renoir, a Cézanne, a Rembrandt. There were also photos of two kids growing older in various locations, young in Mexico, teens in Paris, Adults in London. And there was a photo standing upright on the bureau by the windows. It showed a smiling man, standing in a bathing suit on a beach.

"Well," said Robert, "she was Angela Cooper, aged 46, single mother of two grown kids, Brent 23 and Holly 21. Her husband Howard died in a car accident more than 10 years ago."

"No sign of a forced entry downstairs so she must have known her killer," said Sam.

"Maybe," replied Robert. "M.E. pegs death somewhere around ten pm to midnight."

"And cause of death?"

"Not sure, they are going to be bagging the body and getting it down to Helen right away. I figure it looks the same as with the other one, the Anderson case."

"So now what? Where do we want to start looking?" Sam asked. "We have to go back to the beginning and reexamine everything."

"Yah shit," said Robert. "What about Cummings? God I thought we had him. I thought he was so going down for Connie's murder. Maybe we can connect him with Angela."

"Maybe, but we may have a serial killer, it really only takes two you know. Hey are you in a hurry to go?" asked Sam.

"Well I would like to get back as soon as we can," he replied.

"I just want to look around for a bit more if that's okay?" Sam asked.

"Well make it quick will yah, we've got a lot of interviews and paper work to get through this afternoon."

Sam looked at the photo of the smiling man again. Must be Angela's long dead husband, Howard. He looked like a really nice guy. Maybe not what you would think of as good looking or handsome like Thomas, but Howard still looked friendly.

I wonder how he treated Angela? Did she have a nice life? Happy? Fair?

Sam looked at the pictures of the kids, Brent and Holly. They looked nice and friendly as well. Staring at the camera obviously enjoying their travels, enjoying the company. And sometime today Robert and Sam had to sit them down and tell them how their poor mother was so brutally murdered.

Sam found the room very feminine. The curtains had lace down the edges, the bureau even had a doily on top. Very different feel to something in Samantha's circles of taste. Almost everywhere were pink and white colors. Rich looking room, the type of room where a woman might feel so comfortable and a man so very out of place. It was a stark contrast to have a kneeling dead body in such a cozy place.

It all seemed so wrong she thought as the M.E. started to lay the body out for transport.

What a waste of life, Sam thought. A nice happy family brought down by a monster. She felt tired and depressed. The weight of death weighing her down.

"Okay, let's get out of here Robert."

chapter twenty

Sam sat at her desk tired and exhausted. It had been a long day. Interviews with the Cooper kids, gathering all the evidence, checking through both murder scenes. Cleaning up after death.

The precinct was dark. Most of the lights were out on the fourth floor, Sam sat still in the semi-darkness. She knew what she had to do but she felt guilty doing it. She was twisting some of Roberts hair in her hand wondering how DNA works.

She thought back to the summer at the cabin when she was fourteen. Near the end of the holiday when everyone was out on the beach getting ready for a barbecue. Samantha had felt comfortable and content at fourteen before there were any older Australian friends of Sue's dad anywhere near the beach that year.

All the adults were sitting around the beach in chairs or on the ground, drinking and talking and laughing when Sue and Sam came running down the hill from the cabin, along the dock and dove into the water. Well, Sue jumped in but Sam made the unfortunate decision to dive in. As she hit the water, her bikini bottoms stayed on the top while she slipped under. She remembered the feeling of guilt. Not in the act of losing her bottoms, but rather in what happened next.

No one had really noticed what happened when she stood up quickly and grabbed her bottoms to pull them under. The water was up to her chest as she stood. Murky water. She knew no one could see. So instead of putting her bottoms on right away, she moved around in the water naked from the waist down. She felt so free and alive, her senses heightened, her guilt giving way to thrill of waving and talking with the adult men in the group knowing that just below the water she had no clothes on. So shocking, so naughty, so thrilling … so not like the normal Samantha.

The guilt of the pleasure is how she thought of it sometimes, but more than that she remembered the thrill of it, of almost getting caught. The thrill of the pleasure. That's how she thought of that summer. Young girl's silly thrill.

She looked around the squad room, no one was there. She placed Robert's hair in an envelope, wrote 01) Robert Shore in big bold lettering and slipped it into her jacket.

She moved quietly to the door of her new supervisor, Ron Davis, the Division Area Commander Five. Any guilt gave way to the thrill as she picked the lock and opened the door. She closed the blinds and turned on the desk lamp. She sat at the desk and pulled the main drawer open.

Fuck, just don't get caught was all she could think about while she looked through her boss's personal belongings. Ron was an extremely precise kind of person. His desk drawers were neat, the contents lined up square. Everything seemed to be in its place. Every inch used precisely.

She looked at his picture on the wall, he was standing on a stage getting some sort of award from The Superintendent of Police along with the Mayor of New York. He had just moved to Chicago from New York a few months ago and become her and Robert's boss, one of the five Commanders in Chicago. She decided he was kind of cute in his formal uniform, his naturally balding head covered by his hat so with his slightly long dark hair he looked much younger. Ron was a small man but could be brutally dramatic and loud when he was chewing you out in front of everyone for a mistake. Already comfortable in his new position, he liked to play the bully. Small man complex, she thought, big man mouth.

Another photo showed Ron with his wife and their two boys. Sam was surprised that the photo was still hanging on the wall. Sam had met the boys a few weeks earlier and realized the photo wasn't recent, they were now much older than it showed. Ron's wife was a beautiful dark-haired woman who looked pleasant enough in the photo, but Sam had heard nothing good about her from Ron. All he called her was the bitch and said she was ruthless. Sam had heard a rumor that she was actually his ex, she had run off with his old partner. Sam wondered if that's why Ron called her nothing but the bitch.

Sam started drifting into thought of Ron placing his hands on her stomach and caressing her vulva or circling her clit. Could she imagine him doing anything like that or was all the thoughts just too gross? She wasn't attracted to him at all, nothing, zilcho, in fact he kind of turned her off somehow, he was sort of repulsive in his own bullying 'Ron' way. At least with Robert she wasn't grossed out, just uncomfortable. God it can't be Ron … can it? Fucking gross …

Come on dummy … she shook herself out of her dreams. She only needed some evidence, ignore all the porn magazines, focus girl … get something quick and let's get the fuck out of here …

There was a noise. Someone was walking around in the main room? Oh my God, now what, she thought as she turned out the lamp and sat still, waiting to get caught.

She slowly moved to the window and peeked through a blind. Detective Bruce Taylor was standing on the other side of the room by his desk looking through some files.

He looked up from his desk and seemed to turn and look straight at her. She closed the blind and stood very still.

Fuck, she thought, he can't see me can he? Isn't it too dark? She waited and held her breath. She opened the blind slightly. Bruce was walking around his desk and out of the room.

She managed to slip out of the office, quietly closing the door and sat down at her desk just as Bruce returned from the photocopy room.

"Oh I didn't see you there Sam," he said when he walked back to his desk. "What are you doing here so late?"

"Just finishing up," she answered as she stood up and stretched.

"I'll walk you out," said Bruce. "Just let me lock my stuff up."

You're next, thought Sam. I will be breaking into your shit soon enough.

Two o'clock am and Sam lay wide awake in bed. She was exhausted but couldn't really sleep. Too many things were buzzing through her head. The murders, evidence, DNA, her captor and his gentle hands, her body reacting to his caresses, Angela and the horror of her lifeless face ...

What if Sam was next? She really needed to know if both Connie and now Angela had been tortured before death. Had they been put through weeks of this game that she was being put through? Weeks with multiple and very intimate intrusions ... violations of their bodies and souls ... humiliating visits by some sort of what? Monster?

Wait, it was torture wasn't it? Was it torture? She didn't know. And she didn't dare tell anyone. Who was the monster?

Christ, she thought, I don't want to play this game anymore! I'm scared and I want it to stop ... but ... but ...

Thomas would be home from Washington tomorrow, fall into safety my dear.

She reached down and placed her right hand between her legs and clamped it hard up into her crotch and fell asleep dreaming of Thomas.

chapter twenty one

Alex was swabbing the open mouth gag used on Angela when Sam walked into the lab.

"Hey Alex, I got some of the samples you wanted."

"Not now Sam," Alex whispered, "too many people around. Just leave them on my desk. Don't forget to mark them, so we know who they are."

"Okay," Sam lowered her voice, "but I was really hoping you could get started early ... like today ... I'm just starting to get really worried. It's freaking me out with the murders. First Connie, now Angela ..."

Alex hugged Sam and gently whispered directly into her ear.

"Samantha," Alex said, " everything is going to be alright. You are safe. Nothing is going to happen to you. You are surrounded by dozens of Chicago's finest."

"For the first time in quite a while, I think I'm really scared ..."

"I know," said Alex, "and I am sorry but I can't process anything during work, just come back later and we'll start going through them tonight."

"See you at six," said Sam as she threw the two envelopes onto the desk and turned to walk out of the lab just as Robert was walking in.

"Hey partner," he said smiling, "you beat me in this morning, there's a first."

"Ha ha," Sam stuck out her tongue at him. "We can't all be perfect like you …"

She looked at Alex's desk. The two envelopes were clearly visible with their big bold lettering scrawled across each surface. One marked 01) Robert Shore and the other 02) Ron Davis.

Fuck, she thought, what to do?

"Hey Robert look what Alex has for us," she said guiding her partner away from the desk and over to the counter where Alex was standing.

"Well I don't have much yet really," Alex glared at Sam. "I just started to swab the gag and bindings and stuff."

"Okay, well we'll leave you to it then, let us know when you do," Sam said quickly. She turned blocking Robert's view of the desk.

"Just a sec," Robert said. "Have you had a chance to go through any of the finger-prints yet?"

"Nope sorry. Plenty of prints too … left all around the room. It's going to take a while Robert, I'll call you or text you if I find anything."

"Okay, thanks." Robert turned to Sam. "Let's go talk to Helen and see if she has figured anything new on the death."

"Coming," Sam smiled and let Robert lead them out of the room. She turned to glance at Alex who was putting the envelopes into her top drawer.

"So have you talked with Thomas yet?" Robert startled Sam with the question as they walked down the hall to the elevators.

"What?" Was all Sam could get out.

"You know, about your trouble sleeping and that maybe you guys need some sort of counseling or whatever."

"We don't need counseling Robert," Sam sighed as they got on the elevator. "I keep telling you … everything is fine … we just need a vacation."

"Yah don't we all," Robert replied loudly as they reached the street. "Your car or mine?"

They found the coroner, Dr Helen Ducat, bent over the body of Angela Cooper putting the last of the stitches in.

"Hey Doc," Robert waved. "How are you doing today?"

"Great," Helen replied. "Been to a Cubs game lately? I'm taking off early today to take Jason."

"Fun, fun, fun," said Sam, "Love to go but no time lately. Can't wait to get back there though, Thomas and I love the dogs … and the beer." She smiled.

"So Doc," Robert sat down on a stool, "What-cha got for us?"

"Well, I have found a couple of interesting things … things that I didn't notice on your earlier case, you know the Anderson vic."

"So does that mean they weren't there or that you just didn't notice them?" Robert asked.

"No, they were there all right. I went back and double checked. I just didn't notice them at first because I wasn't looking for anything like it. Sorry."

"No need to apologize Helen," Sam said.

"First off, we know that both women choked on the nylons that were lodged deep down their throats right, asphyxiation was the cause of death." Helen pointed to the corpse's throat.

"Uh huh," said Robert.

"And their noses were held shut as they struggled to breath, just in case. But today I found traces of lubricant in both victim's mouths and numerous scratches with traces of latex in the pantyhose, as well as their throats. So you know what this means right?"

"Condoms?" Sam asked.

"Yes," said Helen, "and so now I realize that the pantyhose weren't just shoved down their throats. They choked on the killer's penis while he shoved in the pantyhose over and over again. He used the same kind of condom each time."

"Choked while giving a blow job," Robert looked surprised. "God that is unique. Anything unique about the condoms Doc?"

"No just a common brand. You can get them almost anywhere."

"Shit," he said.

"Jesus," Sam mumbled. Oh my God, she thought, it's horrible. What a degrading way to die. What a monster this killer was. Both ladies kneeling naked in front of their killer, hands tied behind their backs and choking while the asshole shoved pantyhose down their throats with his cock. One sick psychopath.

Sam suddenly felt dizzy and had to sit down. She stumbled over to an empty stool and sat down hard.

"You okay Sam?" Robert asked.

"I'll be okay in a minute," she answered.

"And again with Angela here," Helen continued, "no sign of rape or recent penetration of any kind."

What the hell was this guy up to? Sam wondered. What was the point of these killings? Their only suspect, Barry Cummings ... was he the madman? Or was he just trying to throw them off by covering for the murder of Connie with Angela's murder? What a waste. Why was Angela picked?

"Okay, well thanks Doc," Robert said. "Let us know if you find anything else."

"Sure will do."

chapter twenty two

"I'll meet you back at the office," Robert said as he pulled up behind Sam's car to drop her off.

"Sure," she said, "I just have one stop to make on the way back."

After Robert drove off, Sam turned her vehicle around and drove down to the water. She parked and walked over to the benches.

She desperately needed to clear her head. She kept having the horrible images of Connie and Angela being forced to suck on some guy's penis in their last moments while he killed them.

Such evil in this world, she thought. What kind of brutal monster puts someone through that kind of thing? And such a waste of life. Those two women, Connie and Angela, so much more to live for ... to have some total asshole shit head come along and snuff them out, and in such a cruel way too.

We need to find this psycho and stop him, she said to herself. Am I in his crosshairs? What's he doing to me? Is he the one playing me like these two victims, preparing me for death after he's finished toy-ing with me?

Her cell phone rang breaking her thoughts.

"Thomas," she sighed.

"Hey honey, I'm home," was all Thomas needed to say.

She melted and tears started rolling down her cheeks. Oh God, she thought, I have to pull myself together, I have to stay strong. She wiped away the tears.

"Thomas, I'm so looking forward to see-ing you tonight … how was Washington?"

"Good overall … you know the usual crap," Thomas said chuckling. "Hey what time are you going to be home, I have a surprise for you."

"Ooohhh," she toyed, "I love surprises …"

"Well just don't be too late then will you …" He said. "See you later, stay in touch."

Sam was still smiling as she pulled into the parking area near the station. She felt light and easy as she walked into the squad room, until she saw the look on Robert's face. He rolled his eyes toward Ron's of-fice.

"Okay you shit heads," Commander Ron Davis walked into the middle of the squad room and waved all of his detectives together. "Briefing, now!"

"First off," he said, "I just got off the phone with Regional Director Stewart and Special Agent Talbert of the FBI. They said they would appreciate our help with this case, their resources here in Chicago have been stretched to the limit this month with the bombings and those three high-level government kidnappings. So they want us to take point on this one and just keep them abreast of the situation."

"Wow there's a switch," Robert whispered.

"And yes, they have agreed with us, Chicago now officially has another serial killer."

"Ya the penis pervert," someone whispered. Someone else snorted. Another snickered.

"Shore," Davis looked at Robert, "you and Dahill are heading this one up. Taylor, Clark, Hernandez and Shapiro will back you up and help with your fill ins. Everybody else will keep their eyes and ears open and let us know if they hear anything. Clear?"

Everyone in the room were shaking their heads in a collective yes, when Sam had a thought and spoke up.

"Sir, who is going to be in charge of the press, do we go through the FBI or our usual channels?"

"Good question Dahill," Davis said, "this is sensitive so everything, and I mean everything, has to be cleared through me okay? Is that understood?"

Again the heads shook yes.

"If I hear of anyone releasing anything to anyone even remotely hinting toward the press, that person is going to be personally strung up in front of the Mayor's office by his balls, got it!"

Someone cleared their throat. Sounded female, thought Sam as she smiled slightly.

"And we want this guy quick people, understood? We have to get him off the street before the press gets wind of it. I do not want anyone labeling this shit head as the BJ or blow job killer ... the families will go nuts."

"That's for sure ..." said one of the guys.

"Now one more thing, who's interviewed the Cooper kids?"

Robert put up his hand.

"We did," Robert answered. "There really wasn't much, they hadn't talked with their mother for a few days. Neither of them had heard of any lovers, strangers or anyone else hanging around."

"Okay," Davis said. "Let me have your report as soon as you can. Good luck everyone." He turned and walked back into his office.

"Well," Robert turned to Sam, "now that is good news ... the FBI letting us run point."

"Um ... yah I guess," Sam said quietly. She wasn't sure she really wanted to stay on the case.

chapter twenty three

"Hurry up and unwrap it will you," Thomas said quickly.

"Please don't rush me," Sam retaliated sticking her tongue out at Thomas and rolling her eyes, "it's not everyday I get a present from Washington marked Smithsonian Museum."

Both Sam and Thomas were sitting at the kitchen table naked. They had both just stepped out of the shower and were barely brushing each others lips in light kisses when Thomas excitedly pulled the package from his coat hanging in the front hall.

"Just hurry up slowpoke!" he said smiling.

She unwrapped the gift slowly not knowing what to expect. Not really expecting anything. Thomas didn't normally buy her gifts on his trips. He was so excited … he was so cute when he got excited, she decided as she looked up at his face, she was so happy, so in love, so safe.

Sam began to tear up, just a little … as she got the box unwrapped and opened it up. Inside were a pair of handcuffs.

"Cool huh," Thomas said, "they are replicas of the cuffs Houdini sometimes used for his early escapes. I got them from one of the gift shops at the Smithsonian. See watch …"

Thomas took the cuffs and clicked them onto his wrists. In one swift motion he twisted the cuffs counter-clockwise and then clockwise quickly and both wrists came free.

"See … really cool huh … you try it Sam." Thomas tried handing her the cuffs.

A whole flood of feelings washed over Sam as she began to tear up. She covered her face with her hands.

"What the …" Thomas dropped the cuffs on the counter by the stove and hugged her tight. "Please baby, what is it?"

She slowed her breath and began to gain control. She couldn't let him see her like this. She could handle it … couldn't she? She didn't need to worry him.

Come on girl, she thought, you are strong … toughen up … let's see some balls girl …

"Nothing Thomas," she said finally. "They are really funny … thanks."

Thomas smiled weakly and picked her up in his arms.

"You are the most beautiful creature this side of the Smithsonian," he said smiling as he carried her upstairs to bed.

chapter twenty four

Thomas slowly entered Sam as she lay back and thought to herself how she was going to enjoy every second of this intimate time with him.

She reached up and placed her arms around Thomas's neck as he began to slowly pump. She pushed Thomas onto his side but kept her legs wrapped around him. They lay beside each other becoming one mass moving together closer and closer each pump. After a couple of minutes there was barely any motion at all.

Sam held Thomas close, hugging him extremely tight. She wouldn't let him slip out or even loosen his penis from her grip. She wriggled a bit, she knew she could bring him off without even letting him withdraw.

She moved her hips back and forth in a rocking type motion and could feel him inside. God that felt good, she thought, this is the feeling I have missed for so long.

She slowed, then rocked fast. Slowed again, then fast. Moments of safety, she thought, moments of bliss.

"Oh Sam," Thomas whispered as his body shuddered and he came, "I love you."

She held on and rocked a few more times. Then she stopped, but held him tight. He didn't seem to mind. He wasn't moving. She could feel him relax inside of her, but she still held on.

They kissed deeply and she finally loosened her grip a little.

"I love you too," Sam said and smiled as she kissed him on the end of his nose, "you are my oxygen you know …"

"Well if you've breathed enough of me," he said as he nuzzled his face into her neck and kissed it several times. "Can we go make dinner?"

chapter twenty five

The third victim's name was Tricia Palmer. She had been found early Saturday night in room 20 at the run-down Spritzer Motel in the south.

"She's younger than the first two," Robert said.

"It's like there's no pattern," Sam said, "First Connie was married, no kids, then Angela with two kids, no husband. Now Tricia. She looks young and fit like some sort of trainer."

"And he's escalated his timeline. First two were over a month apart, this one has just been three weeks."

Same MO again, thought Sam. Same naked body held upright on her knees by the bed, hands tied behind her back, eyes covered by a mask, mouth held open by an open mouth gag, pantyhose shoved down her throat.

Poor Tricia, thought Sam, so young, what a waste. How did such beauty end up like this?

"Looks like the same MO," she said looking around the room.

"Yup," said Robert. "Hey come and take a look at this." He was bent over looking at the carpet by Tricia's feet.

"It looks like she put up a bit of a struggle, doesn't it?" Sam bent down to join Robert's gaze.

"There is blood on her wrists where she struggled," he said, "but look at her nail … she may have scratched our killer just a tad."

Sam could see some sort of build up under Tricia's left baby fingernail.

"What a break Robert. This is the first time isn't it? The other two must have been overpowered right away but Tricia here put up a fight. Way to go girl, you may have just revealed your killer."

Sam shuddered as she stood realizing she had been talking to a corpse. Without seeing Tricia's eyes she had forgotten, just for a second, that it was a real human behind the mask. Sam walked around the room trying to get away from the body. She examined the walls and surrounding furniture. Plain television on a wire stand with a broken remote sitting on top, two chairs - one with a ripped cushion, cheap bureau - no open drawers. There was a thin heavy greasy film coating everything … no shine ... no sparkle ... nothing reflected any light.

Death had not yet started to become the prevailing scent. The room still smelled of grimy dust and mold mixed with fish, like some sort of horrible underground market.

Nothing in the bathroom at all. Not even soap or those tiny shampoo and conditioner bottles that motels normally like to shower their guests with. Two towels - unused.

What a horrible place to be the last place on earth that you get to see ... what a waste, thought Sam. Washed out and age-faded material, along with dull surfaces of metal, wood and glass sucked all the color out of the room.

She pulled back the window curtain by the door.

"Medical Examiner is here."

"Okay," Robert said. "Hey partner after we get the forensic team in here, what do you say to a little dinner?"

chapter twenty six

Burger and fries again. Some day, she had told herself, you'll have to start eating better. She took another large bite of her burger. They sat in the corner booth at the Hot'n'Spicy Diner.

"So what do you think Robert?" Asked Sam. "Do you think Cummings can still be doing all this?"

"I have to think so," he replied. "The bastard seems guilty to me."

"But I just can't figure out his motive," Sam said. "Is he just covering Connie's death so we won't think it's him?"

"Nope I think he's getting off on it. After killing Connie, he realized he loved it. So now he's finding other women and getting his jollies off killing them as well."

"Well I'm not so sure," said Sam. "Anyway, we have to pin down that nurse at his mother's home and get his alibi straightened out … one way or the other."

"Well if it isn't him," Robert said, "we have a real fucking problem … we don't have any other suspects … the Commander will be pissed."

Sam shuddered as she thought of her own problem. She was scared to have

Thomas go away tomorrow. He had mentioned that he had to return to Washington for only a day or two. That will be enough, Sam thought, you'll be in Washington while your wife's body is being played about like an instrument. An instrument of naughty torture … an instrument of intense pleasure … but what if the serial killer was toying with her just before tiring of his game?

She felt faint and dizzy. She sat with her partner across from her, her husband at home. But she never felt more alone.

chapter twenty seven

Sam sat in the kitchen with Thomas. After such a late dinner with Robert, Thomas had waited up and made her some tea.

"Tea ok?" he asked.

"Yes it's fine," she smiled, "Thank you and thanks for waiting up."

"I don't mind," he replied. "Hey, how's Robert doing?"

"Great I guess. He says hi … he seems to think that you and I are having marital problems."

"What? What gave him that idea?"

"Just you being away so much, I guess," Sam replied.

"Hey I told you."

"I know, I know," Sam sighed, "things will change in the spring."

"Then I'll be home a lot more Sam."

"Well Robert thinks that you're away so much by choice," she said, "he's just concerned that's all."

She sipped her tea and looked at Thomas. Could he be leading a double life? Was he visiting someone else every time he went away? He was always so secretive. He would never tell her where he was actually going or what he was doing.

How much do I really know about him? Sam thought. Didn't Mom always say I'll never know everything about a man? I'll probably never know him completely. How much can you really know about anyone? Look at Mom and Dad. For years Mom didn't even realize Dad was secretly stashing away a fortune until the day he retired and they took off to travel the world.

What secret was Thomas hiding? Or secrets?

"I just wished you didn't have to go in the morning ... that's all," she said.

"Hey why don't you call up Mel or Nat? You need to get out ... have a girls night out?"

"I don't need a girls night out, I need my husband home."

"You've got to loosen up ... you know ... relax." He smiled. "Let go a little in life ... you take things way too personally ... you take life too seriously."

"Fuck you."

"Ah Sam," he pulled her up into his arms. "I love you ... you know ... my little fuzzy peach."

"Fuck you ... she said again. She smiled and kissed him.

They went to bed but didn't make love. Sam just needed to be held tight.

chapter twenty eight

Darkness. Totally black and thrilling. Every inch of skin aroused. Ears drowned in exotic music. The smell of candles.

Her fear biting down on her adrenaline, searing her nerves. She was thrown off kilter, she was naked and strapped down … just as secure … just as open … only this time she was upside down, laying on her stomach with a pillow under her lower belly. Ass sticking in the air.

Fear was pulling at her. What was he going to do now? She lay very still waiting for his actions. He sat on the edge of her bed and stroked her back, up and down from shoulders to her lower back. Slow rhythm, drifting, dream like.

Her body jumped, what little room it could in her bindings, when his hand reach under her and found her left nipple. He rolled it in his gloved fingers, pinching it slightly and squeezing her breast with his hand.

Oh God, she thought. Here we go again … the ultimate pleasure … starting again … his play toy … his torture … his whims … but to what end … to what in return? Murder? Death?

She let her mind wander. Why was he doing this to Sam? Why not just kill her like he had with the others? Did he have some horribly nasty plan for her later after showing her all this pleasure? Showing her all the ways that lovers can please each other and take away all their dignity without making them feel small? He seemed to respect her but at the same time he had stripped her of all her layers and any masks she wore. He knew just what to do to make her forget who she was. She became piano wire in his hands ... an orgasmic tense and tight humming string ... an instrument of aroused tension so turned on that she didn't want to care about anything else anymore.

She had to find out when the three victims first met their killer. Were they all being tortured for weeks before like she was?

He reached under her and found her right nipple. She was spread on the bed with him pressing down on her, both hands reaching around to her breasts. For a very brief moment she lapsed into a thought that she felt even more exposed than before. Her ass was sticking up in the bed, strapped down tight to the pillow. She felt his knee push between her ass cheeks and spread her open.

She wanted to push back, to have his knee press harder against her ass. She tried to move but couldn't. He slowly pushed his knee down and into her. Her ass welcomed his pressure.

Oh my God, she thought, it felt so naughty, so good. He moved his hand down and reached around her lower belly touching her clit with his fingers. She became wet as he started to circle his fingers.

He withdrew his knee and sat back pulling his hands away. She jumped as his hand reached straight between her legs and he pressed his thumb into her while gripping over her clit with his curled fingers. She gasped as the feeling intensified, sucking all the air out of her. His hand withdrew and moved up to her ass and massaged it slowly, circling one cheek then the other.

Suddenly without warning, he smacked her ass. First the right cheek, then the left. The flood of emotions filled her eyes inside her mask. She felt her facial cheeks flood with blood. She felt helpless as she lay blushing at the shock of being spanked. She turned her head away, in case her mask and gag didn't cover the redness she felt in her face.

He smacked her again. Not hard blows, just deeply affecting. She was confused.

How could a simple light blow cause her so many different feelings. She was a tough cop, wasn't she? She had been beaten up lots, pushed around, even punched hard many times by her colleagues in training, but it was never like this. She felt humiliated and yet extremely aroused all at the same time. Tears rolled down her cheeks under her mask. Tears of what? Fear? Anger? Joy? Happiness? Absolute relief? Some sort of passion released deep inside her.

She realized she was not really in pain, at least not much. Just enough to remind her that this was about passion. The hand came down on one cheek, then the other, then both.

She felt more and more receptive as the spanking continued. Any pain was not even felt, she knew she could take much more. It became thrilling, such a naughty desire.

Oh my God, she thought with each slap, more ... give me more ... harder ... you can spank harder ... punish me ... I feel the need to be punished ... you can punish me please ... I deserve to be punished ... I want to be punished ... oh God ...

She was so tense, she felt she was under water, sinking deeper and deeper into darkness.

Her memories drifted and popped around her clouded head. She remembered back to when she was eleven or twelve. She was with her Mom and Dad camping in the mountains at a family reunion. All of her cousins, aunts and uncles were sitting around the campfire one night late when one of her uncles decided it was time for her to learn a lesson, or so he said. For no reason at all, he suddenly snatched her arm and threw her over his knees. He pinned her there while he spanked her. She couldn't move. Her flailing about did no good, he was too big. Even her aunts tried to come to her rescue, at least two of them, the others just laughed. After what seemed forever in her head, he finally let her go and stood to get another beer as she dropped to the ground.

She ran off to the beach with tears rolling freely down her cheeks. The guilt and humiliation of it all. So ashamed.

Sam let go of her memories and let her body melt into the bed. She began to let the pain and guilt of the spanking mix with the feelings of her new found pleasure. She realized how much her old feelings of guilt, shame and humiliation had now turned to a delicious burning desire and intrigue for more. Was that normal?

The spanking increased as each nerve coming from her ass felt the tension roll out ... spreading up along her back to her head and down her legs to her feet. She started to feel incredibly sensitive. As if fire was touching every part of her body.

She felt drained. Her body so tense.

How did this pain become her pleasure?

He stopped spanking her and rubbed her ass lightly. He moved his hands over her lower back and up to her shoulders and massaged the knots out. His hands moved expertly, releasing her tension inside her shoulders and moving down to her ass. Then he moved to her legs and rubbed them up and down hard three times each to release some of the knots.

Then he smacked her ass ten more times pausing between each smack to see she didn't move in a way that showed she was in too much pain. She felt like each time he spanked her, it drove her deeper and deeper into a dark world of desire that she didn't even realize she longed for.

He reached around and pinched both nipples again. She relaxed and felt like she could finally breath.

But then her breath quickened again as he slipped his thumb back in her vagina and circled his fingers in front, over her clit like he was grasping a bottle. He started circling and pumping his thumb in and out, clamping hard the front wall of her vagina between his thumb inside and fingers in front.

She felt so incredibly turned on, so alive, so free. And yet she felt so vulnerable, so helpless, so sensual, laying fully exposed to his touch. She came quickly, her body shaking from her quiet orgasm.

She drifted off amongst thoughts of pleasure and pain.

chapter twenty nine

She awoke. How long?

Her finger freed her but she found it slightly awkward this time. Being on her front, getting rid of the straps around her ankles and across her back.

"Fucker," she said out loud as she twisted around.

She stood and looked at herself in the mirror. Red ass, she flushed in her face again. Red ass - red face, she thought, how touching - matching ends. I never thought pain could carry so much pleasure. It felt so refreshing and cleansing to be rubbing her sore ass.

She cleaned up the bedroom, candles out, music off. She put away the straps, gag and mask into the back of her bottom drawer. She had to make sure everything was hidden away, couldn't let Thomas find it. He'd be crushed to think he couldn't even protect his wife.

After she had finished tiding up, she re-membered she never got the chance to place a glass of water on the bedside table as per Alex's instructions. This time he had caught her a little by surprise, she was in the kitchen when he knocked her out.

Damn … next time, she thought, I will get you then bastard.

After showering, she wrapped herself in her bathrobe and went down to the kitchen. The fading afternoon light drowned the room in dark shadows. She left the lights off and sat and found her cell on the table. She thought about making a call to Melissa. But instead she sat at the table and drifted off in her thoughts.

Her old Captain, when she first graduated from the academy and joined the force, had a saying he used all the time. Every case has a small detail, just one small detail, a tiny little piece of evidence that everyone else overlooked. Find it and you break the case wide open and turn up all the answers. But what was the one little detail in this serial case that she had to get a grasp on? She shook her head to clear it and called Melissa.

"Hey are you busy tonight?" Sam asked.

"What did you have in mind?" Melissa asked, "You don't have to ask me twice, Matt is just laying around watching football all day."

"Sunday night … girls night out?" Sam asked.

"Sure, what about Nat? Want me to call her?"

"If you can, please," said Sam. "I'll come around and pick you guys up in an hour or so okay?"

"See you then."

Sam sat alone in the dark kitchen. She felt lost.

chapter thirty

She could tell she had too much to drink already and it was only 7:30 or so. Melissa and Natalie had suggested going to one of their old hang-outs, Jenkins Pub for dinner and beers. Sam loved it there. Loose and loud, the room cocooned in old whiskey smelling wood, sports on the televisions behind the long bar. Plenty of laughter and beer.

She realized she would have to leave her car for the night. She could walk to it early in the morning just down Southport.

"Ah, fuck that," Natalie said. She leaned toward the others. "There is no way any guy is going to get me to swallow. It's just gross."

"It's not that bad Nat," said Melissa. "I can think of worse."

"Yah whatever," Natalie said. She waved at the waitress for another round. "Most guys don't give a shit really, they just want to see your face down there bobbing up and down … power trip … I tell you."

Sam laughed as both the other two women pretended to hold onto heads in front of their crotches giving them blow jobs.

"And really," continued Natalie, "if it was up to them I think they would rather come all over your face anyway." She laughed and gestured to her cheeks with her fingers.

Sam laughed and leaned over slightly to rub her backside. She felt warm inside and out. It felt really good being out with the girls. Just hanging out, no worries, no killings, no pain and not having to think about or justify her hidden desires.

"Gotta go ... ladies room ... anyone else?" asked Melissa.

"I'll come," Sam said.

"Good I'll wait here for the next round," Natalie said.

They made their way to the back of the bar and squeezed through the doorway to the hall for the washrooms. Melissa was walking fast, Sam had problems keeping up. As Sam passed the Gents door, a guy staggered out. Large guy, large arms, tattoos and smelled of Rye and smoke.

"Hey you," he slurred. He reached out to correct his fall and caught Sam on her right breast. He held on.

"Hey," she yelled slapping his hand away, "what the Hell ..."

"You feel good," the drunk staggered. He smiled and reached out again. This time he had both hands around her waist, squeezing her stomach and hips. "What do you say to a little quality Marv time huh?" He moved his hands up to both her breasts.

Sam froze, she stood undecided what to do. She was trained to take this asshole down but was hesitating. She didn't know why but she felt stupid and in shock. Should she hit, kick, yell for help, negotiate with the guy or beg him. Break both his arms or just beg him to leave her alone. Her body was being abused enough already. It is not my fault Thomas ... it's not my fault. Thomas ... where are you?

"Is there a problem Samantha?" Brad, the bartender, entered the hall. Brad was bigger than the drunk. Taller, bigger arms, ex-NFL, one of the hunks you read about. That's how Sam thought of him since she had first met him years ago. She liked Brad, she always thought he was hot.

He grabbed the drunk by the collar and turned to the front. "Excuse me," Brad said to Sam as he walked the drunk out toward the front door.

Sam found Melissa, already exiting a stall.

"Fucking drunk," Melissa said after Sam told her what happened.

Sam looked down at her shirt. Both breasts and her waist were covered with wet handprints. Sam and Melissa looked at each other and suddenly started laughing.

They were still laughing a few minutes later when they got back to their table, Natalie wondered what had happened.

"I saw Brad throw the guy out," she said. "Asshole."

"Boy, that Brad's a real hunk huh?" Melissa said looking over at the bar.

Sam and Natalie turned to look at Brad.

"You should tell him your available Nat," Melissa said "or we'll tell him your available ..."

All three women laughed.

As Sam stared over at Brad, a sobering thought hit her and her laughter slowed. Could it be Brad Jansen's hands all over her in bed?

What did she really know about Brad. He seemed stable enough but he always found the time to flirt with the ladies. Like the true bartender, always there to hear anyone's troubles. Dreamy body, Sam thought. The perfect specimen. She imagined Brad's hands lightly brushing her nipples and slowly circling her vagina ... her secret lover. Brad sitting on her bed toying with her like a ..."

"Sam," Melissa snapped Sam back as she slapped her glass back down on the table, "snap out of it girl … you're drooling."

"Sorry," Sam said, "just thinking of Thomas."

"Sure, sure," Natalie said. They all laughed.

I have to get Brad's DNA somehow, Sam thought. She excused herself and walked up to the bar opposite Brad. He was drying glasses after they travelled through the dishwasher. His body glistening with the steam and moisture from the dishwasher.

Hunky was the perfect word for Brad, Sam thought, he was made to model. Underwear … small underwear … small, tight, white briefs …

"Need anything Samantha?" asked Brad.

"Thanks for the help back there Brad," Sam said. She leaned into the bar hoping to see something personal of Brad's behind the bar.

"No big deal," he said. "Stupid asshole, he was in here all afternoon, I probably should've kicked him out of here hours ago." He smiled.

"I just didn't want any trouble," Sam said. "I didn't want to start a fight."

"Anytime Samantha," he took a wad of gum out of his mouth and crumpled it into a napkin and threw it in the garbage bin at the end of the bar. "Hey where is Thomas tonight? Girls only huh?"

"Yup," Sam said, "and he's back in Washington anyway."

"Ah saving our world."

"No, not like that at all," she replied, "he's with European diplomats or some-one like that."

She smiled and then bent over to pre-tend to tie her shoe. Fuck, she thought, forgot I wore slip-on pumps tonight.

"You okay," Brad asked.

"Yes, fine, fine," she answered as she stood up again. But Brad was already walk-ing down to the other end of the bar to serve some customers.

Sam took a napkin and wiped her mouth. Crumpling it, she pretended to throw it into the garbage bin. Of course she missed and had to reach down to pick it up and place it in the bin. She switched napkins with Brad's already in the bin and pushed his gum into her pocket as she straightened.

"You look proud of yourself," Natalie said as Sam returned to the table. "He's that interesting to talk to? Remember you're married right … I'm the one who should be talking to him … but who cares about talk, I'm the one that hasn't been laid for months."

And they all laughed again.

chapter thirty one

"So now where to ladies?" asked Sam as she tried to look at her watch. She couldn't read the time. Someone had hit the blurry switch.

They were in a taxi on their way to Natalie's apartment. Out of the three, Sam was definitely the furthest gone and Melissa the least.

"It's after ten," Natalie said. "I have to get home, I have to work tomorrow." Natalie was a dental assistant in the Medical Center. But she seemed to spend most of her days researching new European breakthroughs in dentistry for her bosses. "Thanks for the night out girls …"

She climbed out of the taxi and waved to Sam and Melissa as they drove off.

"Okay Sam," Melissa said, "your coming home with me … you're in no shape to get home."

Sam didn't argue. She followed Melissa out of the cab and into the brick house. Melissa and Matt lived in a nice house a little south of Wicker park and east of Natalie's apartment. Sam had met Melissa years ago while on a case about a crooked lawyer and they had immediately hit it off.

Melissa was a paralegal, who worked for a small law firm downtown. Matt was a welder who worked over in the rail yards so Sam thought they probably had plenty of cash flow for their large house and equally large mortgage. They didn't seem to be suffering.

Matt was laying on the couch snoring. The television was still on, the news on the screen.

"Matt," Melissa said as she shook him, "come on to bed mister … lets go." She led Matt to the stairs and was back in the room moments later holding a blanket and pillow.

"Here you go," she said. "Goodnight, sleep tight." She disappeared upstairs.

"Thanks." Sam took off her jacket and sweater and slipped out of her shoes.

Luckily I'm wearing my comfy panties tonight, she thought. She shook off her jeans and fell onto the couch and pulled the blanket up to her chin. She smiled as she lay looking out at the glow of the street lamp in front of the house.

She felt so safe and secure on Melissa's couch. No one knew where she was tonight. Her secret lover couldn't kill her if he couldn't find her.

She slept deeply and carefree. She was walking through her precinct with no clothes on. Naked except for her Bedford stilettos and the cross her mother gave her when she was young. She entered the homicide division. She swung the door open slowly and waited for everyone in the room to notice she was naked.

She walked up to a couple of detectives, she stopped and pointed to her shaved pussy. When she looked down, she noticed she had a tattoo of a pistol pointing down her crotch. Each one of her colleagues seem to look away as she passed them. No one in the office seemed to pay any attention to her as she walked between them. She passed the girls from the front desk and they just smiled and waved to her.

She sat on Robert's desk with her knees wide apart and waved to a couple of detectives to come and look. She leaned forward and squeezed her breasts together with her elbows. She felt really sexy and let out a purring type of growl.

"I have a break in the case," she said as they approached. "I know who the killer is."

"Yah sure," suddenly Robert was standing in front of her. Behind him was Thomas who was smiling and behind him were her parents who were scowling.

She reached down and parted her labia.

She smiled, "See for yourself ..."

She woke startled. Startled and wet. Morning noises coming from the kitchen. It took her a few moments when she opened her eyes to remember where she was. She also realized then that her panty covered ass was sticking out from under the blanket. She shifted the blanket.

Shit ... a dream ... shit, she thought. What a dream ...

She listened to the noises. Dishes and cups, Two voices could be heard arguing. Melissa's voice got louder as she walked into the living room.

"No I already told you tonight was your night," Melissa said over her shoulder.

Sam sat up on the couch.

"Morning sunshine," Melissa said, "coffee?"

"Yes please," Sam answered.

"Well you looked so cute laying there earlier, I didn't want to wake you. Come into the kitchen, we've got a couple of minutes before we have to go."

Sam slipped on her jeans and followed Melissa into the kitchen. Matt was sitting at the table reading the morning news on an iPad, cup of coffee in his hand.

"Morning," he said.

"Morning Matt," Sam said, "I'm really sorry we disturbed you last night when we got in."

"Hey not a problem sweetie," he winked. "It was worth the view this morning ... nice ass ... nice panties ..."

Sam flushed.

"Oh stop it Matt," Melissa said. She turned to Sam and placed a cup of coffee down in front, "he's just bugging you Sam, he didn't really even look."

Sam stuck her tongue out at Matt as he winked again.

"Perv," she said.

Matt was about to answer but sneezed instead. He reached over to the counter to grab a Kleenex, blew his nose and threw the tissue into the garbage.

"And don't forget it's your night tonight," Melissa said to Matt. "We alternate most nights, you know, whose night it is to cook," she said looking at Sam.

"Cooking? What's cooking?" Sam asked and smiled. "When Thomas is home he does most of the cooking and when he's not ... you know ... burgers. Well that's why God invented fast food ... isn't it?

"Okay we are out of here," Melissa said, "can't be late, come on Matt."

She stopped at the door and looked back. "Make yourself at home honey, shower, whatever, just lock up when you leave."

And then they were gone.

Sam sat at the table sipping her coffee until the cup was empty. She was lost in thought.

It couldn't be Matt, could it? What about Melissa? No, he couldn't do that to her, he wouldn't ... Would he? Could he?

She went upstairs to take a shower.

Half an hour later on her way out the door, she took the tissue out of the garbage and went to find her leather jacket.

chapter thirty two

Sam approached her desk thinking of her weird dream. Almost embarrassed at the thought of it, her inner most private parts exposed to the whole building.

Just a dream, she kept telling herself over and over.

"Hey partner," Robert said as she walked up. "You look rested."

"Yup nice Sunday, how about you?"

"It was ok I guess," he said. "Had any thoughts about the latest murder?"

"No, I thought we should go over everything again."

"Okay, let's go into the boardroom and get started."

"Okay I'll be right there, just give me a sec," she said as she unlocked her desk and placed the napkin and Kleenex in her top drawer and locked the desk again.

They started by laying out everything they had from Tricia's murder. Then they wrote out points on index cards. The entire boardroom was full of evidence from all three murders with index cards pinned or taped onto almost every available surface.

"One," Robert said, "the hotel room had been rented by Tricia herself. She wasn't accompanied by anyone."

"Two," he said, "she told friends early Saturday that she was on her way out of town for a few days. Sounds like someone she knew stopped her from going out of town."

"Or she never was going out of town," Sam said. "She was planning on having an affair in the hotel the whole time."

"But why would she have to hide it from anyone? She's young and single, what would she have to hide?"

"Well maybe not her, maybe the killer had something to hide," Sam said as she reached for the crime photos that the technicians had printed out.

Robert's phone on his desk rang, he ran to answer it. "Detective Shore," there was a long pause, "okay well thanks anyway doc … it was a good try."

"That was Helen," he said as he slumped down in the boardroom. "The scrapings under the victim's nails were from coated leather. Probably from one of the pieces of S & M gear that the bastard was using to restrain her."

"Fuck," said Sam. "I thought we had nailed the son of a bitch."

"Yah still no slip ups, no evidence any-where, no DNA even."

"Maybe we should go down to the motel and start asking around again," she said. "Maybe somebody saw something and just forgot to tell us."

"Okay let's go … I'll drive."

chapter thirty three

Sam was at her desk again, after they had spent most of the day walking around the motel asking witnesses about Saturday.

Her shoes were off and her feet were tucked up under her in the chair. The light of the evening was just beginning to fade in the squad room. Detectives and regular officers were packing up desks, slipping on coats and exiting at regular intervals. End of the day exit.

"My feet are killing me," Sam said to Alex on the phone.

"Get better shoes," Alex said.

"Hey I just got these new Somer running shoes and they're the best, just that we did a lot of walking today."

"Any new evidence?" Alex asked.

"Nope," Sam said, "absolutely nothing … zilch … complete waste of time … nobody … saw … anything …"

"Well there is nothing new here either. So speaking of which, have you got any more personal samples for me?"

"Yes," Sam said, "I've got a couple more but if you can wait a few more minutes, I can maybe grab one or two here and bring them all down to you tonight."

"Okay, not a problem, I'll wait for you."

Sam straightened her legs in her jeans and kicked her running shoes under her desk. She looked around the room and sat patiently while the last three officers packed up and left.

She walked across the squad room and sat down at Bruce's desk. Bruce Taylor was a quiet type of man. Very polite, but quiet. Probably in his late twenties, his light hair was slightly longer than most of the others. He wore it really scraggly and Sam always thought it made him look younger than he was. He was cute though in that school boy sort of way and his hair allowed him to go undercover quite easily. Just let his whiskers go for a few days with some dirty clothes and he was a completely different man.

She always wondered what it would be like to kiss Bruce. She would sit in thought when they were having department meetings and dream about making out with him. It was her little secret fantasy, nothing she would ever really do … just that he was so damn cute …

His desk was a mess just like his hair. Papers and files were stacked all around his laptop. She looked around the room again and then bent over to pick the drawer lock.

"And that's when the bitch punched me …" Tony said to someone behind him as he walked through the door. He and Frankie walked in and laughed loudly.

Sam ducked. What the fuck, she thought. Panic! Now what am I supposed to do, what if they see me ducking behind Bruce's desk. Stupid idiot, why didn't I just stand up and move away?

She lowered herself down off the seat and crouched down behind the desk. Quietly she sat on the floor. She began to sweat. A lot.

Fuck, she kept thinking. Fuck, fuck, fuck. What if one of them comes over this way, what can I say? I have absolutely no sane reason for sitting behind this desk. Fuck.

She waited on the floor while it sounded as though Tony and Frankie sat down.

"So then what happened? Frankie asked.

"I decked her," Tony answered. "Fucking bitch tried to take me down, fucking rights I decked her. Put her out cold … she was still out when I brought the bitch in."

"Fucking bitch," repeated Frankie.

Both men laughed.

Sam placed her head on her knees and sat very still. She let her mind wander. She thought about the time when she was fifteen or sixteen and almost caught masturbating in her bedroom.

Her mother and father were having a party at the house with all their friends. She had been out most of the evening with a group of her own friends just hanging around. Sometime after eleven they broke up and all went home. She had gone into her bedroom and was sitting at her desk with her back to the door when she started thinking about a couple of the boys in the group.

She reached down under her sweater and unzipped her jeans and moved her hand over her crotch. She started rubbing herself and thinking of the boys. She hadn't ever really masturbated before so she was unaware of anything she should be doing, she just kept rubbing. It felt really good and she was just starting to really enjoy herself when suddenly her bedroom door opened and her neighbor Mister Phelps was standing there. She immediately withdrew her hand and covered her crotch with her sweater. She flushed and felt the wave of humiliation wash down her body. She felt horrified and really ridiculous, frozen in shame.

He said how she should join them downstairs at the adult party. She made an excuse that she would come down and join the party in a few minutes. But she sat rigid, staring straight ahead at her desk. She didn't dare turn around and look at Mister Phelps.

And even though she knew he was drunk, she always wondered if he saw anything. Had he ever known what she was doing under her sweater?

She shook herself out of her thoughts. What time was it?

The squad room was mostly dark, only a couple of fluorescents were left on. She peaked out from behind the desk, but no one else was in the room. She sat up at Bruce's desk and picked the lock to his drawer. Inside was just as messy as the top of his desk.

She found a couple of used toothpicks in the top drawer which she placed in an envelope and locked up the desk. She moved to Phil's desk and thought how easy he had made the collecting. He was one of the last surviving dinosaurs, he still smoked. She stole two of his used cigarette butts from his portable ashtray.

She walked back to her desk and sat on the corner, wondering about Phil. Phil was almost the opposite of Bruce, his partner. Phil was short, black, slightly overweight and had the hint of going bald very soon. As if he would wake up tomorrow morning with no hair. He smelled of strong aftershave, covering many other smells, Sam thought. But at least it wasn't the same strong cologne that her secret lover used. She relaxed a bit when she thought that at least her secret lover couldn't be Phil ... wait ... could it? He wouldn't be changing colognes just for each of her attacks, would he?

He couldn't, she thought as she slipped on her running shoes and grabbed her jacket.

chapter thirty four

Sam walked in just as Alex was reaching for her phone.

"God I thought something had happened to you," Alex said, "I was just going to try to call you."

"Sorry," Sam said, "Got held up … here's the next four samples." She handed Alex four envelopes. On them were written names in bold, black lettering. 03) Brad Jansen, 04) Matt Harper, 05) Bruce Taylor and 06) Phil Clark.

"Thanks, I'll process them as fast as I can and let you know."

"Thanks Alex," Sam said. "I'm really sorry but I didn't get a chance to put out the glass of water by my bed before the last event."

"My God it happened again?"

"Yes just like the other times," Sam lied.

"Geez maybe you should put in a bunch of cameras to catch the bastard."

"I can't start tearing up the house and dropping in closed-circuit cameras everywhere. What would I ever say to Thomas to justify it?" Sam asked.

"What about a hidden IP or pin hole camera, like a hidden webcam?"

"I don't know, let me think about it."

"In the meantime," Alex said, "I have the results from your first two samples, they were both good reads. You even had the guts to bring me something from Ron?"

"Well I have to rule out every guy I know," Sam said. "Oh and by the way, Matt's sample here, I just threw it in to be on the safe side. He's really happily married to a girlfriend of mine so he better not be cheating on her or I'll kill him."

"Okay, I'll run him just like the others."

"Oh and I have a swab of my mouth and a separate one of the gag he's been using so you can check for whatever it is he's using to knock me out." She handed Alex the wrapped swabs.

"Great, I'll get on it as soon as I can," Alex said.

"Thanks Alex, you're the best."

Sam left by way of the alley just in case anyone was still in the lobby at night.

chapter thirty five

"What do you feel like, red or white?" Thomas asked.

"I don't care whatever you'd prefer," Sam said. She really never knew which she wanted red or white. She usually just left it up to Thomas whose choice always seemed to pleasantly surprise her.

"So you looking forward to the show tomorrow night?"

He had been away in Boston most of the week and had returned just in time to fly her to New York Friday night for dinner and spend Saturday exploring the city before the stage show he had promised. They were staying at the Plaza for the two nights.

Sam had really enjoyed checking into the Hotel. She appreciated being with Thomas at times like that. It was the little things, he always made things seem like such an adventure. They were off to explore another city, staying in a beautiful hotel in the heart of all the action. Sam felt special and sort of secretive, no one really knowing where they were or what they were doing.

After they had checked in, they walked around and found a small cafe on West

57th that offered a variety of casual foreign food to add to Sam's adventure. They had sat by the window on the second floor, the perfect view to people watch as New Yorkers hurried about their evening.

"I've always wanted to see it, you know that. The Phantom of the Opera has been running for twenty five years."

"Yah, yah, well it will probably be a couple of hours I'll never be able to get back," Thomas smiled.

"Fuck you," she said and punched him. "Try to enjoy it will you ... for my sake."

"All right," he leaned forward, "I'll try, just for you." He kissed her lightly on the cheek.

"Thomas," she whispered, "I have to ask you something."

"Shoot." He sat back and waved his hands open in a large exaggerated arc.

"I have to ask you something seriously," she said quietly.

The waiter approached and placed two menus on the table. He listed the specials and left with an order of a modest red Italian wine which Thomas had assured Sam she would like.

Sam watched Thomas as he talked with the waiter. Thomas had such an ease to him. Such a comfort. He was calm and friendly with everyone, she decided. He always seemed to know what to say in any situation. He was always so sure of himself. She loved him so much sometimes it seemed as though her chest ached. Now was one of those times as he reached for her hands and looked into her eyes.

"Now what is it you want to know?" He smiled.

How can I even think of asking? Of course he loves me, she thought. He is mine … and only mine.

"… Ah nothing," she hesitated. "… It's nothing …"

"Ask me anything Sam, go ahead, try me."

But she couldn't. She quickly changed the subject and they began a deep conversation as to the merits of organic versus processed foods in North America and Europe. After dinner they had sat at the table until late, playing one of their favorite games. Since their forth or fifth date years ago, their usual pass time was to sit and make up extravagant stories about complete strangers they saw walking by.

Numerous times Sam had introduced the idea of a male leading a double life with two wives or a wife and a mistress, but Thomas never seemed to flinch or change from his pleasant, smiling self. He was the rock of confidence. Her rock.

The next day they had spent the hours walking around some of the main attractions in New York. In the morning Sam had started off feeling a bit lost in the big city, but Thomas soon made her feel at ease. He knew exactly where to go and what to show her and was having fun making her day a real adventure. He seemed to know the city well. She wondered how many other cities he knew so well.

Saturday night, sitting at a long table in the Plaza food hall, Sam was scanning the room for anyone famous. She had heard that they were spotted there once in a while and she didn't want to miss her chance seeing anyone. Long counters, bright lights and swift moving waiters were all she could see.

Sam was wearing her classic black cocktail dress and Thomas had on a black suit, white shirt and black tie. She knew they looked like a real couple, they suited each other both in looks and style. She felt so spoiled sitting in the Plaza, waiting for their oysters and crab.

"So how was your week?" he asked.

"Not bad I guess," she said. "It's just that we haven't really moved ahead any further on our latest case and I'm not sure where we are going with it."

"You'll get through it Sam," Thomas said, "I just know you will. Now tonight's all about you. Let's forget all about your case, no worries of work. Now tell me how everything else is going?"

What to tell him? Sam thought. Where can I start? Come on, think. Focus, get a hold of yourself. I can handle this, I don't need to worry Thomas, he'd go nuts finding out his wife may be falling in love with a stranger's hands.

Was she falling in love with those hands? Is that what her feelings were? She looked at Thomas and wondered what she could say. After she caught the bastard, would she ever be able to tell Thomas how the psychopath had toyed with her, had played with her body for weeks and used her completely for his pleasure … oh wait … all her pleasure … whatever … small details wasn't it? The point was some psychotic asshole was using her as a sex toy whenever he wanted to, and what was worse she was beginning to fall completely under the stranger's spell. Those hands … the pleasure … the pain … the release … when would he finish with her and then just kill her? Would she die just like the others?

"Fine," she answered. "Melissa and Natalie say hi by the way."

"So you went out the other night?"

"Yup. Those two are such a riot. I may have to go out like that more often," Sam smiled.

"I'm Jealous," Thomas said.

An hour later, after a bottle of expensive wine, many oysters and some crab, Sam started to feel a little light headed. She shook her head and forced herself to focus on the night. Nothing was going to ruin tonight, she decided. She hugged Thomas's arm tight as they left the hotel in search of a taxi to take them to the Majestic Theatre.

In the darkness of the theatre, Sam hoped that if Thomas noticed, he would think her tears were only for the Phantom.

chapter thirty six

"So how was New York?" Alex asked.

"Nice," Sam answered. "The show was incredible, and the hotel was beautiful. We had a very nice time."

They were sitting in the building's cafeteria over lunch. It seemed that most employees either ate their lunches at their desks or went outside more nowadays. The room was almost empty.

"So did you talk to Thomas … you know … about things?"

"No way," Sam defended. "I told you before I can't tell him anything. He'd kill me."

"Well you know my opinion, I think you should tell him and get it over with."

"No it would crush him. I'm not going to put him through that. I will solve the case and catch the guy and Thomas never needs to know what I went through."

"So," Alex said, "I have isolated all the compounds he has mixed together to knock you out each time … very sophisticated stuff."

"What is it?" Sam asked.

"It seems that it's some sort of arial spray filled with a mixture of proposal, ether, thiopental sodium, flunitrazepam and gamma-hydroxybutyric acid. Knocks out a person in seconds, leaves them out cold for five or ten minutes and then awake with no lingering affects and absolutely no side effects. Really advanced stuff. I think Russia used to play around with this kind of spray during the cold war."

"But I don't understand," Sam said, "how could Barry or anyone else I know get a hold of this stuff?"

"Beats me, but at least we know he isn't hurting you in the least," Alex said.

"Bastard, wish I could catch this guy." But inside Sam wondered if she even meant that ... those amazing hands ...

"And so far the DNA samples have all been strong," Alex said, "I have them all mapped but of course no matches yet. You need that glass of water to nail this fucker."

"I'll put it out on my side table just in case. So far all of the events have happened after Thomas was gone, but who knows."

"You never can tell what opportunity this fucker's going to take ... or what he's thinking ..." Alex said.

"Although I'm pretty sure he waits until he sees Thomas gone before he comes in the house," Sam said. "Or maybe he even knows Thomas's schedule. Could it be someone Thomas knows?"

"I thought you ruled that out a long time ago, it has to be someone you know … and fairly well too."

"You're right," Sam said, "it has to be someone I know. He seems to know me a little too well."

chapter thirty seven

Valerie MacLean was frozen in the same position as the others. Hands tied behind her back, mouth forced open by the same kind of gag, eyes hidden behind a leather mask.

Sam looked around the room. The large living room made up most of the rich suite in one of the upper floors of the new North Front Tower. Floor to ceiling glass looking out over Lake Michigan.

This time the killer had been sitting on the couch probably admiring the view while his victim was being forced to suck on his penis and have her nylons stuffed down her throat. Sam shuddered as she looked over at the victim. All this beauty, she thought. And all this evil. What a tragic end to what looked like an exciting life.

The pictures of Valerie hanging around the walls showed the woman standing with all kinds of celebrities, both male and female. She looked as though she knew a lot of famous people.

Officer Tate walked over to Robert and Sam. He had already explained to them that he was the first one on the scene.

"The victim's name is Valerie MacLean," he said. "She was a big shot producer in the motion picture industry. A producer of big budget films around Chicago. She has been divorced twice, both husbands live in LA. The call came in around 7:22pm by a Wendy Tillman, the maid. I arrived at 7:28pm, came directly upstairs and was let in by Ms Tillman. Nothing has been touched and the Medical Examiner has asked me to let them know when they can move the body."

"Just give us a few more minutes," Robert said, "we shouldn't be long. So what do you think partner?"

"Definitely our guy," Sam said. "Everything's the same, victim, MO, lack of evidence, everything except the fact that the door looks forced."

"Yah weird that," Robert said, "it's as though Valerie opened the door to talk with our perp and he had to smash past her chain because she suspected something and wouldn't let him in."

"Or he didn't have the time to wait, maybe someone was coming into the hall."

"That could be a break," Robert said, "we can ask around to see if anyone caught a glimpse of him."

Sam examined the desk and found a couple of unopened envelopes. Turning them over she realized they were probably scripts sent to Valerie in the hopes of being read.

"Hey did you notice a computer at any of our last crime scenes?" Sam asked. "I don't think I remember seeing one anywhere."

"No I don't remember seeing one either, why?"

"Well I would've thought out of any of the ladies so far, this victim would have had one sitting on her desk at all times hunting through emails." Sam checked under the desk and pulled out an empty plug on an ethernet cable. "I'll bet a laptop usually sits here. We're going to have to go back and see if any of the other victims are missing their computers as well."

"Well spotted partner," Robert smiled, "this could be our big break."

Sam found herself in the bedroom wondering if Valerie had been sleeping with anyone recently or if she had many lovers. It seemed as though there were all sorts of candidates up on the walls but who knows? Sam thought, you can never tell nowadays who's with who. Who's intimate and who's not.

Sam heard Robert release the body to the Medical Examiner. She stayed in the bedroom so she could avoid seeing Valerie's body again before it went into the Coroner's body bag.

She looked around for the laptop and any other evidence in the bedroom and bathroom. Very expensive taste in furniture, Sam thought, and very nicely decorated too.

After she had heard the noise die down in the living room, She walked back out and stood by the balcony door looking out over the water. She thought about Valerie and her last dying breaths. Poor woman. All this wealth and fame and in the end, nothing. Nothing could stop a monster from taking her down.

Sam suddenly stopped breathing. It was as if her heart stopped as well. Into her focus had come Robert holding a bright red scarf.

"This was found under her coat on the far end of the couch," Robert said.

Sam stepped out onto the balcony and let the cool night air bath her in silence.

chapter thirty eight

Sam stood in the quiet night high above Chicago. She tried to regain her breath. Slow, in and out, she thought. Just in and out. Just stay alive long enough to …

"You okay," asked Robert. "You look kinda funny, kinda pale, you know?"

"I have to go Robert, I'll meet you tomorrow and we can go through everything then okay?"

"Sure partner," he said, "no prob. See you in the morning."

Sam drove along the water and stopped at the park. She locked her car up and walked slowly out to the beach, past the park, near the edge of the water. She turned her cell phone off and started walking aimlessly along the water.

She felt paralyzed somehow. Was this all with fear? She wondered. She was going to die and she couldn't tell anyone. She couldn't let anyone know how she felt. Tears rolled down her cheeks as she walked slowly along the water. She didn't dare tell anyone now, they would kill her … how could she have let it get this carried away?

Yesterday, she had almost talked herself out of worrying that her secret lover was the same monster who was killing all these poor women. And then Robert had to pull out the scarf. That fucking scarf, same as the one left in her bedroom the first time she was held captive.

She passed a young couple walking the other direction. The woman was holding onto the arm of her boyfriend ... husband ... lover ... whatever. Sam thought of Thomas and wished she had told him everything after that first encounter ... but now it was too late.

She remembered back when she had just joined the force. She had been on the streets for only a few months when she had accidentally run into a fairly big situation. A hooker had run up to Sam one night on Saint Clair and asked her for help. She followed the girl into an alley and realized too late that she had been careless. Her partner didn't even know where she was, he had just walked across the street to get a cup of coffee.

She stood alone in the alley with the hooker and a dead body at her feet.

"You got to help me," the girl pleaded. "He was going to kill me."

"What's your name?" Sam asked.

"Angel," the young girl answered.

""'I'll call it in," Sam said but before she could reach for her radio, a hand grabbed her arm.

"Don't move," a deep voice said very close behind her.

She felt her entire body go stiff with fear. Wait, she thought, wait … don't kill me … this shouldn't have happened … I just forgot for a second … I shouldn't be here …

"Come on bitch," the voice said and grabbed the girl, letting go of Sam. And then they were gone, leaving Sam in the alley alone with the body.

She stood stiff and didn't move. What the fuck just happened? she thought. Did something just happen that shouldn't have?

She slowly looked around. No one was there. How long? One minute? Five minutes? Longer? She shuddered and reached for her radio to call in the find.

When she talked to her partner she lied by saying that she had just stumbled upon the body herself. Sam never told anyone of that night.

And her guilt rose inside even worse when they had discovered the body of the young hooker four nights later. Sam had pretended to have never seen her before. She couldn't let anyone know she had ever talked to Angel … it was too late. She had felt so guilty, that one mistake had bothered her for years, but she hadn't thought of it for a while. Not until now, Sam thought of her guilt.

She walked along the water lost in thought. Her shoes were wet and sandy. Her jeans scraping along the sand gaining weight from moisture. People were thinning now and she could only see a few younger males scattered about on the beach.

The night air was fresh and cool and dark. She began to realize she probably shouldn't walk any further into the night. Fear started to grip her chest. Her breath shortened. She turned and started to walk faster back to her vehicle.

Wait, she thought. I am a cop … a full detective … I can handle a few punks. Can't I?

She walked very quickly back to her car and drove home. When she found Thomas in bed, she crawled in and hugged him tightly while she tried to sleep.

chapter thirty nine

Robert followed Sam into the the ME's office.

"Hey Helen," Robert said, "What-cha got for us this time?"

"Same stuff mostly," Helen said. "Choked to death on her nylons. Obviously stuffed down her throat and in the same way by a condom covered penis. At least my guess is a penis, otherwise why use an open mouth gag."

"Anything else?" Sam asked.

"Not really, still no fingerprints anywhere. And I still haven't found any trace of DNA, anything other than the victim's. But I have noticed a couple of things though …"

"Like what?" asked Robert.

"All of the victims do range in age by quite a bit, between twenty five and fifty two, but they are all in good to great shape and they all kind of look alike. Dark hair, attractive and all natural brunettes."

Robert looked up at Sam. "Like you," he said.

"Yes," Helen said, " Kind of like you Sam."

"Been talking to any strange men recently Sam?" Robert smiled.

"No," she turned away. Not talking to them anyway … if only I could say, Sam thought.

"Well let's drive over and see if the boys in the lab have anything new," Robert said.

Before starting the car Robert turned to Sam.

"You know, the bastard is killing sooner and sooner. The last two weren't even two weeks apart."

"I know," Sam said. "I was thinking that. It looks like his need for this gruesome ritual is increasing."

As they entered the forensics lab they were almost overrun by Director Dale MacKetchison coming out.

"Oops sorry," Sam said as she caught Dale's arm when he passed. But Dale never responded, he just hurried out the door. Jerk, she thought.

"So how's everyone today?" Robert asked looking at a couple of lab techs, Paul and Vince.

"Fine," they responded in unison.

"Anything new on the case?"

The tech named Paul motioned Robert and Sam over to a table. On it were several items from the case.

"Here's the mouth gags," Paul said, "all have been checked for trace but nothing found. No trace of clothing or any other materials. No DNA other than the victims, nothing. And the bindings around the wrists and the necks belong to each of the victims, they were found at the scene by the killer and used out of convenience, that's all."

"Where would he be getting all the gags? Robert asked. "I wonder if we could track down any purchases?"

"Doubt it," Paul said, "so far they have all been different makes. They've probably been ordered from different places online. Could be dozens of suppliers and no red flags, one gag ordered from each."

"Damn," Robert said.

Alex motioned for Sam to join her at her desk. Sam walked around the room over to Alex.

"Got anything more," Alex whispered.

"Not yet," Sam whispered, "no time."

Robert was still talking with the two technicians.

"I just wished it would all go away," said Sam, "I think I'm starting to get a little worried."

"Oh Sam, I think we're getting close … but if you can't handle it …"

"I'll handle it," Sam said.

"Well everything we got so far is all good but of course still no matches," Alex whispered. "Anyway we are going to have to be real careful from now on, I think MacKetchison is starting to catch on."

Robert walked up behind Sam.

"Hey Robert," Alex said.

"Anything new?" asked Robert.

"No ... nothing new. I have been running trace on everything I can find but finding nothing."

"All right thanks Alex," he said as he turned to leave. "Just call if you find something."

Sam had to walk quickly to catch up. She caught him just as he reached the elevators and stepped into an empty one.

"So what was that all about?" Robert asked.

"Oh nothing, she just wanted to know where I got my purse."

"Ah right ... girly talk ..."

Sam stuck out her tongue.

chapter forty

The blackness surrounded her again as she opened her eyes. Black. Exotic music playing, same smells of candles mixed with foreign cologne.

She was bound on her back again, spread open, face up, gag already in place. She waited to breath. She didn't want to make a sound. She wanted all this to stop. She worried that soon her time would be running out.What would he have planned for her today?

Her fear was building. She was thinking about the other victims. It appeared that he had toyed with the other victims for a few weeks prior to ending their lives, but there was no real proof of that. He may have tired of the games as well and decided that he had enough.

Try to be very quiet, she thought. She took a slow breath in. Just lay quietly and pretend to still be under the influence of the inhaled drugs.

She felt the electric shock when his gloved hand touched her leg above her knee. He moved his hand slowly up her leg and stomach to her left breast. It found her left nipple and he rubbed over it back and forth. She tried to resist by thinking of the other victims.

What was it that Helen said? Sam thought. They all fit the same kind of body type, all four victims so far had dark hair like Sam's. Sam fit the profile.

His hand reached for her right nipple as his lips closed around her left. He sucked on her nipple, first softly, then harder.

Where's my gun, Sam thought. Downstairs? She had been surprised again by the intruder. This time he had snatched her as she came out of the shower. Thomas had already left early that morning.

She tried to move. Just work your way free, she thought, then you can fight this bastard. But it was no use, her bindings wouldn't give.

His hands moved up to her neck and slowly up the side of her head while brushing her skin lightly and running his fingers through her hair.

Oh god, she thought, I … have … to … fight …

He moved his mouth over to her right nipple and then both hands were rubbing her head. A new type of feeling started to envelope her. She started to feel compressed and smothered, but oddly in a good way. Securely bound, she felt like she was being forced in some way to become part of the bed, to slip into a coma and just disappear into the covers.

He kissed her neck lightly and she tried to breath through the gag. Why was her gag so different? She wondered. Her tongue could again feel the familiar round hard ball of rubber. Was this the one he used to torture his victims and then he changed to the open one when he killed them?

He kissed between her breasts and started kissing down to her navel. His tongue danced and circled around her lower tummy and slowly licked up one thigh and then the other. Every nerve in her lower body began to tense up again. The familiar wonderful energy started to build up in her body.

Oh shit, she thought, I ... must ... fight ... this ... I ... must ... resist ...

Think of the case bitch ... use this time to develop a witness statement. Think of everything you can about this man. His weight, his smell, his hands. Those wonderful hands. Gifted hands. Loving hands. Oh shit, she thought, I am falling in love all over again.

Suddenly she heard an unfamiliar sound. It was some sort of buzzing, a light sort of hum. More panic! What the Hell? What was he doing?

She shuddered as she was touched by the source. A vibrator? She wondered. It slowly moved up her left thigh. She had never felt anything like it. It seemed to make all of her nerves wake up, fully energized.

The feeling was incredible, the vibrator moved up to her navel and then up to her left breast. He toyed with her nipple using first the tip of the vibrator and then the smooth flat side. He rolled it over and around her nipple till it was hard … it felt even harder than usual.

He moved to her other nipple while the humming continued. She felt a warmth envelope her chest, a unique feeling of nerves spreading from her breasts.

He started to move the vibrator down to her belly and closer to her vagina. She felt herself go wet … she could feel herself start to let go. Oh fuck. He circled her clit a few times, all the while keeping the amazing vibrations touching her skin as much as possible. He danced the vibrator around her lips and around her clit. It was heaven.

Suddenly it all stopped. He lifted himself off of her lower body and roughly grabbed her breasts and nipples with both hands. The humming continued but at a distance. Oh god, she wanted him to enter her so badly. She groaned through the gag, monster or no monster, she could not think. She wanted to be fucked. She had to be …

He snapped something onto both her nipples. What the hell? she thought, what is this? Nipple clamps? Aroused beyond what she thought was normal, her breasts felt on fire. Pain gave way to pleasure as her nipples were squeezed harder than she could ever remember. Not quite numbing, but more of a constant reminder of the intense pleasure. Electrifying nerves, she thought, her chest on fire. Amazing pleasure and pain mixed to mess with her mind.

He moved the vibrator around her thighs rolling it slowly up her left thigh across and then back down her right. He moved it over her pubic bone and let it rest right on the bone. The vibrations travelled through the bones at her core and down her legs. Her entire lower body felt like it was being shaken by thousands of hands.

The vibrator only rested on her clit for a few seconds before she came in an explosion. The orgasm hit her so hard, she almost forgot where she was. Oh fuck. She shook hard in her straps.

But it continued. No rest this time … he moved the vibrator and positioned it so that he could enter her. He held it there resting on the outside of her vagina. She moaned and tried to shout, please … oh please … yes …

He slowly pushed the vibrator inside. She tried gipping it from within and was rewarded with a whole new pleasure … a fantastic feeling of intensity was building from inside her, but so intense she had never felt it before.

He placed one hand on top of her lower belly and circled it slowly as wave after wave of explosion blew from her insides. Her mind exploded and went blank. Fuck, fuck, fuck.

The vibrator kept humming, sending continuous shocks through her entire body. Her vagina felt raw with nerves, tightening around the shaft and shooting fireworks outwards. She was hard from her neck down. Tension running through her entire body.

The vibrator was slowly pulled out and then pushed back inside. He kept up the slow pumping, the amazing torture, the warmth of her entire body was numbing, she was on fire, every nerve electrified.

She came again … and then she fainted.

chapter forty one

She awoke. How long?

He was gone, ring on her finger. She released herself and slid the mask off from her eyes.

She didn't move. Her body was stiff as she lay exhausted still bound to her bed.

She lay still watching the candles in the room flicker light and shadows around the dark room with their dancing flames. It smelt of lavender and sex. Her orgasms seemed to now have a delicious smell linked to them. She took a large sniff in through her nose and held it for a few moments before releasing it slowly.

She noticed that the glass of water by her bed sat untouched by her stranger … her mysterious lover … her horrible monster.

What's happening to me? she questioned. What am I going to do? My life has fallen apart. I'm searching for a monster, a killer of all these women, some sick fuck that I have to get off the street. Something I have to stop. Someone I have to kill. But I am letting this same monster do all this to me every time he knocks me out. Am I crazy? Am I fucking nuts? Am I in love?

Can it be love that is stopping me from telling anyone?

This level of intensity was something she had never experienced before and she knew it. It also made her realize she had so much more to learn about herself and her body.

As she lay watching the fractured light bounce around the room, she thought of Thomas. She had first seen Thomas at an art exhibit put on by a friend of Melanie's. The show was hideous as far as Sam was concerned. She could remember how all the sculptures looked like giant penises poking though donuts, she remembered thinking at the time, this is art? This is shit.

While she was standing on the balcony overlooking the gallery, she was approached by a very handsome and well dressed stranger. He looked at her and said how much he admired the artist. Sam was stunned. How can he admire her? she had asked.

He said he admired her so much, he thought her courage was amazing for bringing so much crap out into the world and showing no signs of failure. They both laughed hard at his comments.

They looked around the lower room and commented on how everyone is eating it up. The fabulous art of a mad woman. Then this handsome stranger asked Sam if she felt like going next door for a drink. She had said yes, anything was better than standing around looking at giant penises all night. They had both laughed hard again. It was the first time she had ever done anything like that in her life. Dropped out of an event just to be alone with a stranger. But Thomas seemed so funny and full of life. He seemed like he could take Sam on an adventure as soon as she began talking with him.

They saw each other numerous times that week and started to officially date by the week after. When Sam had introduced Thomas to her friends, they had all seemed kind of jealous, he was perfect they all told her. He was handsome, he was tall, he was kind, and he was funny.

Thomas is my wonderful husband, my lover, my best friend, she thought, but he is always so damn mysterious. And now with these gentle stranger's hands? They have started to teach me there is so much more. And yet when is it all going to end? I have to kill this psycho before he kills me!

She undid the straps. The nipple clamps were laying on the floor. She stood to blow out the candles. She felt light headed and awkward with her stiff body. She felt as though she had been exercising for a week straight. And she was hungry.

The bastard had even left her the vibrator. It lay silent on the bed. Maybe the batteries are dead, she thought. She picked it up and turned it on. The funny hum in her hand made her laugh out loud.

After cleaning up and putting everything away, she opened the curtains in the room and let the sunlight flood the corners. Another beautiful Chicago Sunday evening, she thought. Her body was stiff but felt amazing, she felt energized. Life felt good. She went downstairs to make herself some dinner out of last night's leftovers.

chapter forty two

The gym smelled of the usual sweat and dirty socks. Sam looked around the bright room for any staff.

"Do you know if Axel is around?" she asked one of the girls who walked up to the front desk.

"I think he'll be in around ten," the girl answered.

Sam went into the locker room. She figured if she had to wait, she may as well get changed and start warming up before her workout.

When Sam emerged from the locker room, she almost ran straight into her early mentor. Fay Wallis, a determined woman who went from supervising the Police Detectives in the force years ago to becoming the CEO of a very successful private security company.

"Samantha," Fay said, "what a pleasant surprise."

"Hello Fay," Sam smiled and gave Fay a hug.

"My God, it has been years … I don't think I've seen you since your wedding."

"What brings you to this part of the city … you don't live around here now do you?" Sam asked.

"No but my new boyfriend works here so I changed gyms so he can whip me into shape." Fay winked.

Fay was older than Sam by almost twenty years but Sam always thought she looked spectacular. She was permanently made up and looked as if she rolled out of bed with makeup on and hair in a perfect flip. She was thin and in shape and known to be strong. She held a few of the women's lifting records at the precinct for a number of years, even after she had moved on to the private sector.

Fay had been Sam's mentor when Sam first arrived at the precinct. She was hard and sort of cold at times, but Sam always thought she was fair. Sam was always in awe of Fay.

"So it didn't work out with Roger then?" Sam asked.

"Ha, I left that bum a couple of years ago … he was cheating on me … leading a double life."

"My God," Sam said, "I can't believe it, he always seemed so devoted to you … you two seemed perfectly suited to each other."

"He was a bum ... it's always the nicest ones you have to worry about the most ... right?"

Sam suddenly thought of Thomas and wondered what he was doing right at that moment. He's supposed to be in New York isn't he? He could be anywhere right now couldn't he? He could be playing nice husband to some other sucker female. Number two wife. Maybe he hasn't even left Chicago ... maybe he ... wait ...

"Yah ... I ... guess," Sam said.

"So how is work? Have you caught the killer yet? What do the papers call him, the Stocking Stuffer Killer?"

"Yah that's what his nickname is right now and no we haven't caught him yet. That's kind of why I'm here ... checking on a suspect," she lied.

"Oh my goodness, here?"

"Well it's just a hunch, you never know."

In walked Axel. And both ladies moved toward him. Sam was about to ask him if he had forgotten about their ten o'clock when Fay moved in and kissed him.

"You're dating Axel?" Sam was stunned.

"Well yes, yes I am," Fay said. "He and I met three months ago and almost instantly hit it off ... didn't we Axel ..." Fay squeezed Axel's arm.

"Surprise," Axel said, "I didn't realize you two knew each other. This is hilarious …"

"I'll say - surprise," Sam said. "Ha, well you guys make a lovely couple." Wow a real boy toy, she's more than twenty years older than him, Sam thought. She smiled.

"And Samantha is on the case right now," Fay said. "She said she's here to follow some suspect around in that horrible killer case." She looked around the room.

"Wow," Axel said, "Who's the suspect?"

"No, no," Sam said, "I didn't mean it like that … just running through a couple of leads … nothing concrete …"

"Wow," he said, "someone right around here?"

"No don't worry about it ... Really," Sam said. "So I'll go warm up before our session. Nice to see you again Fay … I'm sure we'll run into each other more now that the two of you are an item."

"You bet," Fay said hugging Sam. "Say hi to Thomas for me … you two are still together right?"

"Yes." Sam said a little too quickly. She walked off to find the area to stretch.

Sitting on the mats, she wondered how the hell she was going to take something of Axel's back to the lab for Alex to examine.

What the fuck was she going to do?

chapter forty three

Sam was squatting on the toilet seat in the second stall of the men's bathroom. She had to keep her feet up so they couldn't be seen and she had to be quiet … very quiet. She didn't want the front desk girl to see her or hear her as the girl made the late evening rounds to close up the gym.

Earlier in the day Sam had decided after three failed attempts to get Axel's DNA, the only way to get it would be to break in at night and take it. While doing her training, she had started off trying to collect his sweat but that turned out too messy and all of the samples would have been compromised anyway. She then turned to a kleenex that he had thrown away but each time when she approached the garbage can, someone would walk by and throw something in before she could do anything. Finally she thought of stealing his water bottle but every time she had the chance to grab it, he came by and picked it up. Finally Fay took a sip of water from it and ruined another sample.

So Sam had returned in the evening to the gym under the pretense of another workout and had in the meantime, scouted out the skylights as a means of escape without tripping the alarm.

She squatted in the washroom, hidden away from everyone … waiting until the gym was closed. What the fuck am I doing? she thought. Is this entire quest worth all this? What if I get caught? Can I really talk my way out of this one?

The girl opened the door, looked around quick and then let the door close slowly as she went off down the hall.

Sam waited about ten minutes before moving. She pulled her baseball cap down low in case of security cameras. She slipped out of the washroom and down the hall to the staff room. She knew the perimeter alarm was set but the back part of the building, where the staff room was, didn't have any sensors. All she had to do was find Axel's locker, remove any item for the DNA test and then escape. She figured she could relax, she had all night. What could go wrong?

As she entered the staff room, she heard laughing out front. What the … wasn't everyone gone?

Sam poked her head around the corner carefully and spotted the girl making out on a couch with her boyfriend.

Oh Christ, Sam thought.

"Oh tell me again," the girl said, "what was she saying?"

"You heard me," the boy said, "she kept saying she couldn't discuss the case every time her trainer asked who the suspect was that she was following. Really creepy stuff."

"Yah but ever so exciting!" the girl said.

Sam flushed as she realized they were talking about her. It seemed even more creepy when she realized she was eavesdropping on a conversation that started by someone eavesdropping on her.

She moved back quietly into the staff room and walked around looking for Axel's locker. She could hear the two out in the front starting to really get serious. The girl was moaning and the boy was grunting.

Locker thirty two, Axel Blaine written on the door. Sam checked the lock. Damn, she thought, combination, not a key lock, no chance of picking it. What to do … how to … she pondered. Wait … check the door. The door, even though locked, still had a lot of play to it … thank God for cheap, thin metal doors. If she could get enough leverage ...

The two young lovers out front were making a lot of noise now. Moaning and groaning. Grunting and swearing.

Sam found a coat hanger and straightened it out. She braced herself by the locker and was just reaching for the door when she heard the girl and the boy move down the hall toward her. Sam ducked behind the middle row of lockers and held her breath. They stopped at the doorway, sounds of heavy kissing and groping. He peeled off her shirt as she moaned loudly, it flew past Sam and onto the floor. Sam moved behind the next row of lockers and stood behind a large vending machine.

"Let's go for a shower," the boy said.

"In a minute," the girl said.

Sam heard a zipper. Then a moan. She waited. She heard the girl start to make love to the boy's penis with her mouth. Sam couldn't see the blow job, but she could certainly hear it. And it was a noisy one. After only a couple of minutes, which to Sam seemed like an hour, the couple moved past the staff room into the shower area.

Fuck, thought Sam. Have to hurry. She braced herself and pulled on the top of the door. She had just enough room to slip the coat hanger in. Eventually after some twisting and turning, she snagged something inside. She slowly pulled it out and grabbed the cloth. She wiggled it out of the locker and held it up. One of Axel's t-shirts, his name on the front. Perfect, Sam thought.

She could hear the lovers in the shower, definitely the sounds of making love. She moved slowly to the front of the gym and out the front door, being sure to hide her face from the cameras.

chapter forty four

"So how are you feeling?" Thomas asked.

"I'm fine, why do you ask?" Sam stood up and walked to the sink. They had just finished breakfast. The kitchen was blown out in bright sunlight and smelled of coffee and toast. Thomas was home for a few more days before another trip was planned to New York.

"Just wondered," he said. "I just thought maybe we needed to talk about a few things."

"Like what?"

"I don't know but what's bugging you? You seem like you are always mad lately and I don't know if it's me or if you are mad at the entire world."

"Oh it's you all right," she said, "I feel like we don't talk anymore."

"I know but every time I bring something up," he said, "you just walk off or leave for work."

"Ha, I am not the one that is always leaving Thomas … you are."

"Yah well hopefully just a few more trips … you know that … and then I will be around a lot more. I'll probably be around so much then you won't know what to do with me … you'll be tripping over me all the time."

"Right," she said, "I'll believe it only when I see it."

She realized she was mad at Thomas, but that it was a little unfair. He couldn't understand her fear and dread every time he went away. Sure, she thought, I get almost an entire day of amazing self-discovery and orgasms, but I worry when it's all going to end … when is the killer going to be tired of playing with me and just end it? When do I wake up with an open gag in my mouth … do I wake up?

Her inner mind kept yelling at her. Some cop! You're pathetic! When are you going to get control of your life? What are you doing to stop this madman? When are you going to stop him from killing anymore? You have to stop this monster!

She went upstairs to dress for work. She stood in the bedroom staring at the bed.

"Come on Sam." Thomas had followed her into the bedroom. "Talk to me, what's the problem … it can't be just that I'm away so much … you know that's going to change."

"I know," Sam said, "I'm sorry … it's just work. I'm just really tired and stressed."

"Well I know I haven't been around much, I haven't kept up with any of the news around here … I don't even know what's going on in Chicago lately. Is it bad?"

Don't say a word, she thought. I can't tell him anything, it won't do any good … just leave it alone. "Nothing your superwoman wife, can't handle."

"Well tell me something about it, maybe I can help?"

"No," she said, "I don't want to discuss it with you." I can't discuss it with you, she thought. "It'll be alright." I will be alright, she thought. "You wouldn't be able to help anyway."

"Oh Sam, you never know," he said as he hugged her.

She hung on tight as she slipped into a numb dream. Thomas felt so safe, so secure, so dependable … she fought off the tears … she hung on tight … she felt so alone.

chapter forty five

Sam called Alex and arranged to meet over drinks at Jenkins Pub. They had arrived after dinner and sat in the back corner.

"So you think you've found the one yet?" Alex asked.

"I'm really not sure," Sam said, "it could be anyone. As you know we have no real leads in the case and we haven't collected any evidence yet at any of the crime scenes that will help us identify any suspect."

"I meant with your own case Sam, have you figured out who has been brutalizing you every time your husband goes away?"

"You make it sound so violent," Sam said, "I keep telling you it's not like that." She remembered the gentle hands stroking her breasts. "I love those hands."

"You what?" Alex was shocked.

"Well I've never felt anything like it before, that's all."

"And now you're falling in love with some maniac's hands?" Alex made a large gesture with her hands.

Is that what she's doing? Sam thought. Is she in love? What about Thomas ... where does that leave him? Can she be in love with Thomas still while loving some stranger's touch?

"So you still think they could be the same guy?" asked Alex.

"I'm getting more and more convinced of it every day. I just can't figure out what his game is though, how long he's going to keep playing me. I just don't know how long I can hold off his death spree ... I just want to match his DNA and catch the bastard before he decides he's had enough with me."

"Jesus Christ Sam, I really wished you would change your mind and tell someone. Tell Thomas, tell the bosses, get them to set up a trap ... tell everyone."

"No way," Sam said, "I'm not going to tell Thomas, especially not now, it would kill him. Then he'd kill me. And I'm not prepared to tell Robert or Ron either or anyone else for that matter. I'd be the laughing stock down at the precinct ... sissy cop ... can't even stop someone from fucking her in her own bed!"

"Hey I thought you said he's never penetrated you?"

"Yah well he hasn't, not technically, not yet anyway ... "

Sam thought about the hands again. The stroking and pinching of her nipples. The rubbing and flicking of her clit. The penetration of her inner most self with his thumb. And the vibrator! He seemed to know exactly what would excite her, it was like she had her own professional sex therapist. She smiled.

They sipped their beer in silence.

"Well anyway," Alex said startling Sam, "like I said before, the samples have all been good so far but no matches yet."

Sam handed her Axel's t-shirt. Alex wrote on the shirt in pen 07) Axel Blaine.

Sam told her the story of almost getting caught by the young lovers at the club. They both laughed hard when Sam got to the part with the sounds of the blow job.

chapter forty six

Robert was on the phone when Sam walked into the precinct. She hung her leather jacket and sat down at her desk. Her inbox had thirty seven unread emails once she got her computer booted up and email opened.

There were numerous emails from up the chain of command regarding policies and procedures, but Sam didn't feel like she had the time to open them. She didn't have any interest in opening them either. Instead, she hit the delete key.

One email that stood out however, was from the nurse at the long term care facility where Barry's mother lived. A Miss Jennifer Delatte had finally replied to Sam's email asking to interview her. She wrote that she had been away for the past couple of days but it would be fine to interview her any time this week.

Sam replied that they would stop by tomorrow sometime after lunch.

Robert hung up the phone and turned to Sam.

"That was the Organized Crime Task Force," he said. "They want us to help

them with one of their busts later this
week."

"Sounds like fun," Sam rolled her eyes.

"Yah, yah," Robert said, "we have to
help those guys as much as we can, their
help has come in real handy in the past if
you recall. I'm just going to go clear it with
Ron." Robert walked over and knocked on
Ron's door. After a moment he went in.

Sam stared into her computer screen.
God if only they could help us catch this
psycho, she thought. Now that would be a
help. But then it wasn't organized was it ...
nothing organized about it. Just a bunch of
random ladies ... Poor unfortunate ladies,
four dead and one still being tortured.

There had to be a connection between
Sam and the ladies somewhere. Sam
opened five separate Explorer browser
windows on her computer and Googled all
their names, one in each window. There
has to be a connection, she thought, I just
have to keep digging.

chapter forty seven

Sam slipped into the darkness of the alley. She had brought her lock picking equipment and a flashlight. Her plan, break in to her neighbor Clarence's garage, find something with his DNA on it and be gone, all in under five minutes. What could go wrong?

She stayed in the shadows as she made her way up the alley. When she reached Clarence and Vivian's house she stopped and stayed low by the fence. She waited. She wanted to make sure no one was home. She peered over the fence and into their back windows.

Satisfied they were out and the house was empty, she found the back gate and entered the yard. Sticking close to the garage, she moved around the front to the small door.

She pulled out her lock picking case and bent down to study the lock. She remembered the free lessons Smiling Johnny Sancho had given her years ago. She could almost hear his voice inside her head. Always try the knob first, you never know when you won't have to pick the damn thing after all.

She tried the handle and it turned. She smiled as she thought to herself, oh good, not breaking and entering, just illegal entry.

She couldn't believe all the junk built up in Clarence's garage over the years. The moonlight revealed stacks of lumber, bits of machinery, old car parts and various other odd looking pipes and valves. Shelves full of the stuff, surrounding the room as well as a maze laid out in the room forcing a person to maneuver back and forth in order to get around. Sam found the workbench on the far wall and started looking for an item she could take back to Alex. Darkness surrounded her as the moonlight didn't reach the far side of the garage. The flashlight danced among the diverse junk forcing Sam to really concentrate at what she was looking at. Numerous times she jumped when her flashlight found a dead, stuffed animal studying her with cold glass eyes.

She finally found what she was looking for, a pair of work gloves, hidden beneath the debris. Just as she was turning to leave a quiet bell and a flash of light caught her eye. She moved between the shelves and into the far back corner of the garage. Sitting on a small desk behind two full shelves was a computer that had jumped to life as it received a message. Sam looked at the photo in the message without even realizing what it was. The realization that the photo up on the screen was of a naked young boy took a long time to sink in to Sam's conscious mind. She shook her head to clear it and suddenly felt sick. Looking around she focused on numerous photos printed out and taped randomly to the wall and to the back of the large garage door. Hanging proof that Clarence Tucci was about to have a shit storm come down on him.

My fucking Lord, she thought. The guy is into kiddy porn! Fuck, now what can I do? Who can I tell? I am definitely not supposed to be in here. How can I find this when I'm not supposed to be in here?

She turned carelessly and knocked over a couple of paint cans that were resting on a small shelf beside her. She picked up the cans and replaced them and then quickly made her way back to the small garage door at the far end of the maze. When she reached the door, she heard voices. She killed the flashlight.

"Well I didn't hear anything Clarence," a female voice said.

"I'm sure I did," a male voice said.

Shit, Sam thought, Clarence and Vivian. They just got home. They must have driven up the driveway on the side of the house, she realized.

Vivian, Clarence's sister, was crippled and in a wheelchair, Sam remembered, they had a specially fitted minivan.

"It's probably just a cat, now hurry up and take me inside." Vivian said.

"Just give me a sec," Clarence answered.

Sam ducked behind a stack of old car tires by the door. She stood four or five feet from the door as it opened slowly and the overhead lights were turned on. A pause. Sam held her breath. Nothing. Wait …. wait. Fuck.

The lights finally went out and the door closed.

"See I told you it was nothing … now take me inside," Vivian said.

"Yes dear."

Sam stood motionless. When she was sure they had entered the house, she exited the garage and went around the side into the darkness. She finally started breathing normally again when she was half way down the alley.

The dogs in each backyard were going nuts as she passed by.

chapter forty eight

Sam and Robert sat in large chairs in a bright, white room at the long term facility waiting for their interview with Jennifer Delatte. A beautiful young black girl entered the room and walked toward Sam.

"Are you detective Dahill?, she asked.

"Yes I am, and you must be Jennifer Delatte." They stood and Sam shook hands with the girl.

The girl smiled. She was beautiful, Sam decided. She looked in her early twenties perhaps. Very slim in her off-white uniform. And a pretty smile … a really genuine smile. Sam had the nasty split second thought that if a woman was ever going to turn lesbian, the beauty of this girl would be the reason that would turn you. The thought passed quickly.

"And this is detective Shore. We just want to ask you a few questions," Sam said, "that's all."

"About Mrs Cummings and her son Barry," Robert said.

Jennifer sat down opposite them and smiled again.

"First off," Robert said, "we have four nights in question and Barry has used the excuse of visiting his mother on three of the four nights."

"Yes," said Jennifer. "He seems to be here quite a bit lately. He joins his mother most nights for dinner and then stays until ten or eleven at night and then leaves. Some nights it's even later, probably a little after midnight."

"Well we know that you verified two nights when our constables first contacted you and you said that yes Barry was visiting on both occasions," Sam said.

"Yes they came and asked me a couple of weeks ago."

"So we know he was here on those two nights, but we wondered about these two as well?" Robert handed her a small piece of paper with the dates of the last two murders on it.

"I would have to go look up the sign in records on the computer. Are you wanting the answer right now?"

"Yes please," answered Sam, "we aren't in any rush."

Jennifer left the room as Sam stood and began to circle the room studying the patients' art on the walls.

"So what do you think partner?" Robert asked.

"Well I don't think we'll see them in any museum that I know of."

"Yah, yah, I meant about the nurse. Think we can trust her?"

"She seems honest enough," Sam said, "I can't imagine what motive she would have to lie to us."

"Not unless she was helping Barry out in any way."

"Really unlikely."

Jennifer returned and sat opposite Robert. Sam stood back and watched her as she handed the paper back to Robert. She doubted there was anything that Barry could ever offer in this world that could make this girl lie for him.

But you never really know people, do you? Sam thought. Motives can come from the strangest of places in anyone's mind.

"Mr Cummings was here on the first date, but not the last one," Jennifer said.

"Do you think he could have slipped out somehow during the three evenings he was here?" Robert asked.

"You know, so no one would know," Sam said.

"Not sure," Jennifer answered. "I guess it would be possible. Go into a patient's room and then wait until everyone is away or occupied and then slip out the back somewhere … but you would have to come back in through the front doors. The other exits are always locked."

"But what if someone jammed one open?" Sam asked. "You know taped the lock. Do your exits sound an alarm if they are opened or unlocked for any length of time?"

"I don't think so," said Jennifer, "I don't think any of them have those kinds of sensors. You could probably just jam the door open and come back in later and no one would know any better."

"And you think there are times in the evenings when no one would notice?" Sam asked.

"Oh sure," Jennifer said. "half the time the hallways are empty. You'd just have to wait until after dinner."

"And what about Barry's mother?" Robert asked.

"Oh she wouldn't notice anything," Jennifer said. "She has fairly advanced Alzheimer's, she doesn't even know what day it is … she certainly wouldn't know when Barry came or went."

"Okay," Robert said as he stood. "Well thank you very much for your help Jennifer."

"Yes thank you," Sam said, "We can see our own way out."

In the parking lot Robert turned to Sam. "So what do you think partner? I figure he could have slipped out any night, done the deed and slipped back in for an alibi."

"Yes, it certainly sounds like it," Sam agreed.

chapter forty nine

Sam realized she didn't like Barry very much. Sam and Robert had found him at home, he was no longer hiding. All three were sitting around Barry's kitchen table. His house was almost in shambles, paint peeling off the walls, linoleum torn in the kitchen floor, broken counter by the sink. The house smelled of cats and dust and the odd pocket of old burnt fish.

Barry was pleading. "I didn't know anything about any of it," he said. "Really."

"Yah well when we talked with you last time, you didn't say anything about knowing any of the other victims," Robert said, "and then we find out you knew Valerie as well."

"But I didn't know her, not really, that's what I'm trying to tell you." Barry's right eye was twitching.

Robert and Sam had earlier decided not to mention anything to Barry about his alibi not panning out completely. They wanted to see if they could trip him up and have him rely totally on the fact of him being at his mother's facility during the time of all the murders. Then they could spring the surprise on him ... his alibi was shit really. He could have left any night that he had planned on killing.

"Okay, Barry why don't we just start from the beginning," Sam said pointing her finger at Barry.

"Valerie's friend Norm told me about a job that Valerie wanted a quote on. She was wanting someone to renovate her kitchen so he had gotten a hold of me. I met with her a few weeks ago but not in her condo. We met downstairs in the bar. After a couple of drinks and some discussion about her kitchen, I left. She had even tried to get me to go up to her place to take a look at the job, but I didn't go. I told her I would be in touch sometime, but I never contacted her again."

"Why not Barry?" Robert asked.

"That bitch was trouble, I could tell … the way she tried to manipulate me into quoting her low … she was trying to flirt with me just to save a few bucks … and I knew she'd be one of those bitches that hovers over you through the entire job always wanting more and more. Hell I even told Connie about her …"

"And after you killed Connie, Angela and Tricia, that's when you decided to go back to Valerie's and make her pay as well, right?" Sam leaned forward on her elbows.

Barry turned toward Sam, his face was very close. She saw his expression change completely and his pale eyes turned cold. She was shocked at the change and fell back into her chair. The look on Barry's face was evil. Absolute evil, Sam thought. He had stopped playing the scared victim and was glaring at Sam with deliberate evil eyes.

"Is that what you think bitch?" He said quietly between his teeth. "Prove it ... you fuck heads."

chapter fifty

Sam sat thinking and dreaming at her desk. Everyone else had gone home. Outside was dark but inside the empty room was still lit. She remembered Barry and the look in his eyes. Oh my God, she thought, he went from playing the scared, little sniveling pushover to a cold, brutal-looking psychopath like someone flicked a switch inside his head. It was so fast it caught her completely off guard. All this time Barry had appeared to be a mild mannered guy when in reality he was probably a cold, ruthless and calculating killer.

They hadn't been able to arrest him, they had no evidence. The only thing that linked him to the murders was he was sleeping with one of the victims and had once met with another victim to quote on some kitchen renovations. Shit, Sam thought, they have to make a connection with all the women better than that.

She was staring into her coffee cup when a flood of memories hit her hard. She remembered the last time she had seen cold calculating eyes like Barry was on a brutal bastard named Kleg. It was back a couple of years when she was taken hostage at a botched bank robbery. The bank memories were so painful for her, she always tried to forget them. She hadn't even thought of them until they suddenly came flooding back. She suddenly felt nauseous remembering.

It was in the hot summer. Sam had been having a long week. She hadn't been a detective very long but was really enjoying it. She liked not having to wear a uniform, she enjoyed wearing her own clothes. She usually wore jeans or slacks and a leather jacket to cover her man-holster and was really proud of her new look. And she always wore practical shoes, usually runners. That came in handy when suspects bolted.

That horrible day, she was wearing the usual outfit … jeans, leather jacket and running shoes. Her gun hidden away under her jacket. Looked like your average retail worker, teacher, maybe corporate secretary on a casual day. She was in the bank waiting in line to cash a refund cheque from a place of higher education, somewhere she had decided not to attend. Robert was back at the station.

The thieves were all standing around the outsides of the room. In unison, they quickly slipped on anonymous masks and announced that it was a hold up. The

popular masks made the bank look like a
sequel to the movie V for Vendetta. They
pulled out Uzis and Heckler and Koch
semi-automatics, along with SIGs and
Smith and Wesson handguns and pointed
them at the bank personnel. One guard
was shot while attempting to pull his gun
in defense. There were eight of the bastards all around the room, that was without
counting any inside informants or turned
personnel. Sam found out about that later.
At the time she had just assumed it was
only the eight of them.

They quickly seized control of the room
and made everyone lay down right where
they were standing to stop anyone playing
hero and pushing the silent alarm. They
really seemed to be well informed and
knew precisely where all the alarms were
situated. Still Sam had not caught on.

After they started moving hostages into
the back in small groups, Sam had begun a
conversation with one of the tellers. A
pleasant young girl by the name of Tamera. Sam confided to Tamera that she was a
cop and had a gun under her jacket. As
soon as she had the opportunity, she would
take down one of the assholes and they
could maybe get word out about the robbery. No sooner had she got the words

out, when Tamera ran over to the thief
that was in charge and started talking to
him while pointing at Sam. Fucking whore
was one of them. The inside bitch, a teller
on the take.

Two masked thieves grabbed Sam and
dragged her into the middle of the room.
Stripping her of her Glock, they padded
her down and found her back up SIG that
was strapped to her lower leg as well. Then
they continued to strip her.

First came the jacket and shoes. Then
her jeans and socks. Then they stripped off
her Butter blouse by literally ripping it into
shreds as they pulled in two different directions. She was crouched down in the middle of the bank trying to hide her almost
naked body. Left with only her panties and
bra, the thieves started laughing at their
boldness.

Then the real humiliation began. They
poked at her with their weapons and made
her stand in the middle of the room with
her arms behind her back. She wasn't allowed to cover herself. She felt completely
naked although her underwear still covered
her somewhat. She stood like that for
hours while the thieves first robbed the
bank of all their safety deposit boxes, and
then while they negotiated with the police

and swat teams on the outside for their escape.

When she had the chance to look into the leader's pale eyes behind the mask, he looked back with a look of death. She later found out his name was Rudolf Kleg, the leader of those ruthless men. His eyes were horribly cold and calculating, no emotion, no feeling, just death. He looked at her as if she was a piece of garbage that he needed to discard as soon as possible. Horrible eyes ... cold eyes ... scary eyes. The same eyes as she had just seen earlier in the day during the questioning of Barry Cummings.

And then near the end of the botched bank job, the worst moments happened. Sam remembered time slowed down for her, she remembered each moment as a slow motion movie playing out in her head. She was grabbed by her hair and dragged over near the main door. Kleg was holding onto her hair tightly as he yelled at the world with all the cops pressed against barricades outside.

We've gotz one of you sons of bitches in here viss us, he had yelled and then Sam remembered the silence as the outside doors were opened slightly by two other masks. Kleg put his arm around her neck and slowly and deliberately opened her mouth with the barrel of his Smith and Wesson pistol. Then pushed her outside into the sunlight. He held her there for a moment, arm tight around her neck, gun in her mouth between her teeth, barrel shoved part way down her throat, her nearly naked body exposed to all of her colleagues in the police force, as well as all the television crews in the city, hence the world. He laughed at his power.

She remembered she had closed her eyes. She knew she was about to die. In that moment in her life, she knew it was all over. Tears streaked down her cheeks as she waited for the end. Anything and everything she knew in life would no longer have her as a part of it. She sobbed quietly as she felt so helpless, she wanted to fight back! But couldn't. She wanted to take these bastards down! But couldn't. She wanted to live and breath tomorrow, but she could see no hope. She remembered she had never felt more scared in her life or even close up to that moment. She was almost weak with fear, she remembered, almost collapsing at the thought of death.

And then all hell broke loose. A sniper took out Kleg with an easy shot to the head. Swat came in from every angle and took the criminals down swiftly and expertly. Only one hostage had a minor injury and the Chicago Police Force was once again cheered by the entire city as the hero of the hour. And it felt good for Sam after the dust had settled and all the thieves were dead, to point to pleasant little Tamera and tell the squad that she was one of them.

But Kleg's eyes had scared Sam so much that whenever she remembered them, she seemed to go weak at the knees. And now she had to deal with fucking Barry Cummings with the same set of eyes!

Sam shivered. She stood and put her jacket on and left the precinct quickly.

She drove around the center of the city until she found what she was looking for, an older hotel with pay phones still in the lobby. She remembered they were secluded along the back wall in the hallway to the bathrooms. Thank God some places have still left these things alone, she thought. She looked around to make sure she wasn't being watched and picked up the receiver.

She dialed 911 and waited for the operator. When the operator answered Sam tried to put on an accent, sort of a German cross, maybe Slavic, but it came out more like a stupid sounding and bastardized version of French or Italian. Either way, it doesn't really matter, Sam thought.

She was quick and to the point. She explained where the police could find the kiddy porn. She gave the Tucci's address and then hung up quickly, not wanting to give the operator time to ask any other details.

She slid out the back door of the hotel and into the shadows of the street. Another good deed done by another good citizen, Sam thought as she found her car and drove home.

chapter fifty one

Sam lay still in the naked darkness, fear had gripped her. Her bindings were tight and she knew she would be unable to move. She wanted to scream but the gag was once again in place. She felt slightly nauseous at the thought of going through this sick torture again so soon.

She breathed slowly and quietly trying not to break the silence. She was annoyed at herself for being so easily taken again. What was that saying about herself? Why would she want to go through this all again? She hadn't really even fought it very much when the hand clamped over her mouth. She had been standing in the kitchen right after she had said goodbye to Thomas and watched him leave. It seemed like it had only been moments later when she awoke on the bed again.

And so she laid afraid of what was coming. It kept running through her head, what did the cold hearted serial killer have planned for today? What weird and wonderful torture did he have running through his head? What was running through those cold pale psychotic eyes? Had he thought about killing her yet? Or was he waiting to use her body a bit more for his pleasure? It was his pleasure wasn't it? Wasn't it? Or was it all hers?

She felt so curious to find out his secrets. The memory of all the other pleasurable times came back to her, it felt strongly of Déjà vu, she felt like she had never really left the bed. All the past stranger's sexual encounters rushed toward her and blended into one big and fantastic feeling of pleasure and pain.

She smelled the lit candles. Exotic music filled the room with thick beats from organs and sitars.

She jumped as the gloved hand brushed across her stomach. He slowly moved up to her breasts. He kneaded first her left breast and then her right. Then both. He started to pinch and play with her nipples.

I have to fight back, she thought. I have to beat these feelings. I can't let this bastard win …

She felt some sort of warm oil drip onto her stomach. The spread of the oil felt so relaxing covering her stomach and breasts. His hands slowly worked the oil into her body back and forth in a mesmerizing circular pattern.

He massaged her entire front from her neck down to her toes making sure to pay particular attention to her breasts and navel and even her armpits. But when ever she thought he was about to approach her vagina, he would pull back a bit and concentrate his motion somewhere else.

Oh God, Sam thought, I am in heaven … no … I must fight …

He rubbed up and down her thighs and calves with the oil and worked out the knots. He then moved down to her feet and spent a long time rubbing and pushing on her feet and between each toe.

Fuck, she thought as her body relaxed entirely. She started to let go and forget all her fears.

No wait, she thought, wait … I must get this bastard … wait …

She drifted into an area where she couldn't remember ever being before. She felt like she was in some sort of trance, her body weightless and floating. Every nerve, every pore relaxed and she calmly drifted in and out of reality. But Sam herself was waiting for the electric tension that could only come from her inner core. Would he release it?

After rubbing down her arms, he slowly moved back to her chest. He began by massaging her breasts and squeezing her nipples. Her inner core started to stir inside and her breathing began to quicken.

He moved down to her hips and rubbed his hands back and forth over her lower tummy. He began to knead the very tops of her thighs and into her crotch and lower tummy.

Sam was feeling divine, her inner warmth building very slowly. Her fear disappeared and she gave way to the pleasure. She moaned into the gag and began to feel the bond again. The bond that had developed between her and the stranger. It had been a long time coming, but had finally surrounded Sam and enveloped her in trust. A deep trust that had developed only through his hands.

She felt all her nerves clinch suddenly when he touched her vagina lightly. Inside she yelled … yes … yes … please … oh please.

He circled around her entire crotch with both hands. He seemed in no hurry to bring her to climax. He moved up and down, back and forth. He pinched her skin around her crotch and pulled on her pubic hair.

She was jumping inside to his touch and began to be overwhelmed by the rush of feelings. It felt like the blood in her entire body had drained into her crotch. Her swollen area became incredibly sensitive to his touch, but he seemed to know that. His fingers lightly brushed around her clit and danced over the entire area.

She felt the sudden pull of her inner lips as his head went down and his tongue began to slowly circle her vagina. Slowly, slowly he licked. His slow light touch was driving her insane, the feelings building from deep within her. Her body tensed up tighter and tighter until it felt like it was going to snap. She felt on fire with tense desire. She needed him inside her ...

She moaned loudly into the gag and tried to reason with him, she wanted him to understand. She needed him now ... she didn't care anymore ... she was too far gone to care ...

The familiar hum began and the vibrator was placed over her lower tummy. He moved it slightly down toward her clit. He circled the area slowly using both the flat of the vibrator, as well as the tip. She moaned again, she needed the vibrator inside, now! But he had other plans.

He rolled the vibrator around her thighs and gently over her vagina a couple of times. It seemed like he was moving slower than usual. He was probably really enjoying the incredible torture he was performing on Sam. He was driving her nuts.

I am going to kill you, she thought, when I find out who you are.

He moved the vibrator toward her clit and that was enough to immediately release all of her fury. She exploded both in mind and all down her body. She shook in her bindings. She wanted to relax but he did not stop. He brought the vibrator down over her clit and let the humming control her vibrations throughout her entire crotch area. The passion and desire overtook her body again and all she felt was a fire of absolute extreme pleasure inside. Her breathing became a series of moans and sighs.

Don't stop ... don't you dare stop, she thought. He left the vibrator humming and propped against her vagina as he sat back. What was he doing? It barely registered with her.

Please, please, she thought, enter me ... I need to feel you inside ... I don't care any-more ...

She heard him suck on his fingers and then he pushed inside her with two fingers. It felt amazing on her humming body. He rolled around and rubbed her on the inside of her front wall. She wanted to grab his

hand and thrust in more. She wanted more
...

Suddenly all her desires were met when he pulled his fingers out and something larger entered her. It slid inside slowly, very slowly. She was so wet ... so on fire with desire ... she tried to grasp hard with her inner muscles.

Oh God, she screamed inside. She gasped and moaned into the gag. It felt so good, whatever was in her felt just right, it filled her so. It slid out and then in again. Over and over, faster and faster. She was moaning constantly into the gag now, almost whaling in desire. Her entire body was over the edge, hard with tension. She was like a tuning fork, high-pitched vibrations sending her over the top again. He suddenly stopped and undid her left hand. He pulled it down to grasp the dildo and started using her own hand to push and pull it in and out of herself. She began a bit slow but soon started thrusting the dildo in and out faster and faster.

She came again hard as her rhythm sped up. Her entire body felt like it was ripping apart. It exploded, leaving her with no thoughts other than the fireworks going off inside her head. It felt like an explosion went off in her brain and cleared it all out.

She grasped at air trying to breath while she withdrew and he took the vibrator away. She could feel her body soften slightly. She lay still, too wiped to move.

She slowly allowed herself to come down from heaven and started to breath more normally. She felt so exhausted but she felt so complete. So utterly satisfied ... So in love? Oh Thomas where are you?

She awoke. How long?

She pulled off her mask and unclipped the gag. She knew she could have ripped off the mask when he undid her hand earlier but she was so involved, she didn't regret not doing it. And she may not have been successful anyway, he may have stopped her, right? she thought. Oh God, what have I done?

She undid the bindings and pulled herself off the bed. Her body felt like it had gone through a marathon and she smiled in the mirror as she said to herself that it had gone through one. A long one, she thought.

She looked around the bedroom and realized that her collection of toys was increasing. A couple of weeks ago she had started to hide everything in a shoebox at the back of her underwear drawer. Somehow he always found it. And now that box was laying open in the middle of the floor. The nipple clamps and a couple of scarves were still in the box. On the floor beside the box was a bottle of massage oil, along with more bindings.

On the bed beside the gag and mask was the vibrator and a new toy Sam had never seen before. She picked it up and immediately flushed. She was holding a full sized, flesh colored dildo, flexible and smooth to the touch.

Oh my God, she thought, I never would have been caught dead with this stuff a few months back. She quickly undid the straps on the bed and threw everything into the box. Back into the drawer it all went until next time.

Sam stopped when she realized what she was looking at. The glass by the side of the bed had been touched. She looked closer and decided, yes he had taken a sip of water from the glass.

Ha, got you ... you bastard, she thought. You are now fucking dead ...

She carefully dumped the glass using a glove and slipped it into an envelope for Alex. Damn, she remembered Alex had told her she was away for a couple of days. Well, I have a nice surprise for you when you get back, thought Sam.

She showered still a bit weak at the knees from all the action. She dressed and left the house wondering what Thomas was doing right at that moment in Boston.

chapter fifty two

Sam walked into the grocery store around 7:00 pm Wednesday night. She usually liked to shop at night when the store was nearly empty and Wednesdays were one of the best nights.

She walked between the bakery shelves pushing the squeaky shopping cart like any normal housewife, pondering whether cinnamon buns were any healthier than chocolate chip muffins, when she heard her name called from behind her.

"Samantha … Samantha," the voice yelled.

Sam turned to realize it was too late to run away. Old Mrs Wilcox was bearing down on her, shopping cart vibrating and making a hell of a racket with its oddly shaped wheels.

"Samantha dear," Mrs Wilcox was breathless and flushed from the brisk chase.

"Hi Mrs Wilcox," Sam said. Thinking if she ran fast now Mrs Wilcox probably wouldn't be able to catch her. Mrs Wilcox was a nosy neighbor that lived three doors down from Sam and Thomas. She had lived there all her life, she was so proud to tell everyone she met. Not quite the age of silver hair and stooped shoulders, but entering that group very soon. Sam had tried to avoid her all summer, it just took the fun out of strolling around the neighborhood.

Mrs Wilcox stood breathing heavy and put up a hand for Sam to wait.

"I … haven't … seen … you … in … ages," Mrs Wilcox finally got out.

Sam smiled. "Just busy Mrs Wilcox."

"Solving all the city's problems Samantha? Getting all the scum off our streets?"

"Well I try," she said and smiled.

"I should hope so dear," Mrs Wilcox said, "there is so much violence these days everywhere. Those poor girls that have been killed lately … and did you hear about poor Mr Simpson?"

"No, what happened?"

"He was mugged right in front of his own house. He beat them off with his cane but they still made off with Baxter."

"Baxter?" Sam asked.

"His little dog … a toy poodle … everybody loved Baxter … he was Mr Simpson's family," said Mrs Wilcox.

"They mugged him for his dog? Geez, what the hell are people thinking …"

"That's all they took ... poor little Baxter ... probably never see him again."

"Hey I have to ask you a really private question," Sam said, "have you ever seen anyone come and go from my house recently?"

"You mean besides Bobby?" Mrs Wilcox asked, "no I don't think so."

"Oh that was a long time ago wasn't it? He hasn't delivered our groceries for months now ... it was back when I was laid up on the couch with that knife wound ... maybe ten or eleven months ago." Sam touched the wound under her shirt as if to emphasize.

"I think he still has the hots for you Samantha," Mrs Wilcox said, "Don't you remember when I caught him that time peeking into your house?"

"I told you, he was just looking into the windows to see if anyone was home."

"Ha," she snorted, "that's what you say, I say he was spying."

"Well that was almost a year ago."

"And remember I overheard him talking to his coworkers, all those other young sleazy boys, he was telling them all about you."

Sam remembered being told that by Mrs Wilcox back last fall. She remembered being kind of flattered at the time, older woman the center of a young man's crush.

"I'm sure he didn't mean anything by it," Sam said.

"Whatever you say dear," Mrs Wilcox said as she launched into another practiced Wilcox rant and rave about city council and changing the parking charges on the main streets.

Sam thought about Bobby. Bobby Braun, probably all of twenty or twenty one. Worked part time at the grocery store between his Engineering classes at the University. Very fit, very good looking. All the young girls came to the grocery store just to hang around and talk to Bobby. He had medium length dark hair, chiseled face, large chin, big biceps, six pack stomach, ripped like the marines as they say. The all around athletic type, Sam thought, the local football hero. Could he be your secret lover?

She imagined him leaning over her naked body running his hands over her breasts and down to her vagina. Inserting his big fingers inside of her and exploring. She thought about those big hands smacking her ass in punishment and feeling her breasts and squeezing her nipples. She pictured him sitting on her bed maybe just in his underwear. Oh God, she thought, he was a pretty dreamy stud ...

"And that's when I thought about decking him ..."

"Pardon?" Sam shook her head to clear her thoughts.

"You know the magistrate ... that's when I wanted to hit him, the stupid old codger ..."

"Oh I see," Sam said, totally lost but not caring.

"Well anyway dear, you have yourself a nice night, I'm off to Jasper's place for some late night Poker. I just stopped in here to get some chips and dip for the game."

As Sam watched Mrs Wilcox walk away she thought to herself, fucking shoot me if I ever turn out like that.

Bobby walked by and Sam was suddenly flustered. She looked down at her groceries.

"Hi Mrs Dahill," Bobby said and smiled.

"Hello Bobby," she looked up. Fuck he was a real looker, she thought, but he was already gone.

chapter fifty three

After gathering her groceries, shopping cart nearly full, Sam found an open till. As she placed the groceries on the belt Bobby came up behind the girl at the till and asked Sam if she needed help taking her groceries to the car. He smiled his usual patented, huge, dreamy wide smile when she accepted.

"And how's mister D?" Bobby asked. They were walking to her car, Sam let Bobby lead while she walked closely behind watching him push the cart full of packaged groceries.

"He's fine," Sam answered, "thanks for asking."

"Good … just wondered … haven't seen you guys for a while …"

"How have you been Bobby?"

"Great," Bobby smiled and looked at Sam. "I'm almost finished school and then I'm outta here." He gestured with his hand flicking his thumb in the air.

"What plans have you got?" asked Sam.

"Big plans … I'm off to London … got hired by an English firm who specialize in overseas jobs … you know Dubai … mostly."

"Wow," Sam showed surprise. "That's great."

Bobby loaded the groceries into her trunk with quick and precise movements. His biceps flexing each time he picked up a bag. Sam was fascinated.

"Well I'll be sad to see you go Bobby," Sam shook his hand. "But I hope you do well over there."

Bobby pulled another huge patented smile and turned to go back into the store. Sam stood and watched him walk through the parking lot back to the entrance. God, what a hunk was all she kept thinking. What an ass. Perfectly round. He's like the perfect specimen of what a man should be like. She again imagined him above her bed stroking her naked body. This time she dreamed he was naked …

She shook herself out of her daydream. Bobby had just reached the entrance to the grocery store when he turned and tore something off of a finger and threw it into the nearby garbage can.

A bandaid! Sam realized. Oh fuck, I could get his DNA, she thought as she climbed into her car. The grocery bags are no good, probably cross contaminated with the girl at the till. But the bandaid would be perfect. Sam pulled her car out and turned toward the store.

There was a private security force vehicle sitting just down from the entrance with the driver watching the doors. Sam had to be careful as she pulled her car along side of the garbage can. She stepped out and could see that she had blocked his view of the can well enough if she could just get around the car without attracting attention. She walked to the back and opened the trunk and peeked around the lid to see if the security guard was looking. He seemed preoccupied with the doors to the store so she stepped over to the garbage can quickly.

No way could she find the bandaid in that mess of papers and containers. What to do? What to do? she thought … she had to think quickly. She looked around at the guard again and then grabbed the entire bag of garbage. She opened the back passenger door and threw the garbage bag onto the floor inside.

Fuck, what the hell am I doing? she thought as she closed the door and ran around the back slamming the trunk closed. She jumped in and sped off not wanting to look anywhere over toward the security guard.

People will think I'm nuts, she thought as she drove toward home. Her pulse started to drop back to normal a few blocks later.

She stopped in the back of the parking lot at the bank on Southport to take a look at her catch. She opened the car door, pulled the garbage bag out and dumped all the contents onto the ground.

Just as she was getting started with the search a squad car pulled up beside her and a regular constable dropped the window.

"Anything wrong?" the cop asked. "Oh hey it's you detective Dahill, anything I can help you with?"

"No," Sam looked up. "Hi Bernie, just going through a bit of a lead, thanks."

"Well you make sure to catch the bastard okay?" said Bernie.

"Will do," Sam said. If only you knew, she thought, I want to catch him more than anyone.

The radio crackled and Bernie grabbed the mike. He answered the call and told Sam he had to go.

She returned to the search of the garbage as Bernie drove off.

After finding Bobby's bandaid, Sam had a thought. She went through the entire bag making sure that the one bandaid was the only one. If there had been any others it would have really made it more difficult and confusing for Alex.

Luckily, there was only the one bandaid in the bag. Sam cleaned up the garbage and threw the whole bag into a nearby can, before heading home.

Driving home, she only had one thought in her head. It sure as hell better be worth it … I hope I can catch the bastard in my bedroom. With all that garbage, my car is probably going to stink for weeks.

chapter fifty four

Sam sat by Alex's desk waiting for her return.

"Here you go," Alex said. She handed Sam a cup of coffee and smiled. "Chicago's finest ..."

"Thanks," Sam said. She sipped her coffee. "So what news have you got?"

"Well I've been through the last samples and was able to pull the DNA okay but just barely, at least on the one."

"Well I got the mother load ... here it is," Sam said. She pulled out the large envelope with the glass in it. "I just hope I didn't ruin the sample or anything."

She placed the large envelope on the desk. Alex picked up a pen and marked the envelope with only the word bastard in big bold lettering.

"And here's a couple more for you as well," Sam said. She placed two more smaller envelopes on the desk marked 8) Clarence Tucci and 9) Bobby Braun. "Although it seems that number 8's real passion is for little boys ..."

"I heard about that. So that was you who called that in."

"Yup, so are you coming to my party tonight?" Sam asked.

"You bet, I wouldn't miss it for the world," Alex said. "Hey have you thought any more about what I said?"

"No what do you mean?" Sam asked.

"You know, telling Thomas what's going on."

"No way, not a hope, don't keep asking me … you know I can't tell him. You promised right?"

"All right, all right … I'll stop," Alex said. "Let's just nail the bastard before anything bad happens to you."

"Got that right," Sam said, "I am getting more and more worried with Thomas being away so much."

"Shit Sam," Alex put her hands on Sam's shoulders. "I think this has gone far enough. We have to catch this fucker."

Sam caught herself thinking, should we catch him? He makes me feel so good …

chapter fifty five

Sam stood by the kitchen door and looked out into the crowd. She and Thomas were hosting a house party and things were really starting to hop. Couples were dancing in the front hall by the living room where the stereo was blasting out some old Astrojet. Others had crowded into the kitchen to discuss various topics from the economy to the latest movies being released.

Most of Sam's coworkers and comrades from the precinct were there, as well as her close friends Melissa, Matt and Natalie. All their neighbors were there with one exception, Clarence and Vivian Tucci. He was in jail and she was probably visiting him, Sam had thought earlier.

But Sam also thought it odd that none of Thomas's friends or coworkers had come. He had assured her that he had invited them all, but she wasn't so sure.

Jennifer, a neighbor walked by Sam and smiled and leaned in toward Sam to be heard.

"Great party Sam," Jennifer said into Sam's ear.

"Thanks," Sam said, "I'm glad you're having fun." Leaning so close, she could smell Jennifer's perfume. She thought it was the new Olivario's Cloud, but she wasn't positive.

Robert caught Sam's eye so she made her way over to the group sitting in the back sunroom. A couple of other older detectives were sitting with Robert and Frankie Shapiro but Sam didn't know them very well. They were all discussing the serial case of course and throwing opinions around in all directions. She stood above the group.

"Well," one of the older detectives said, "I don't think he's local, he couldn't be or why has he all of a sudden appeared? Why now?"

"No idea," said Frankie, "but there could have been any number of triggers that just got him started."

"We'll maybe that's what we should be looking more into," Robert said.

"Hey Samantha what do you think about these killings?" Frankie asked.

"I'm not sure," Sam said, "but I know the guy is super careful, knows what he is doing. He's smart and he's extremely meticulous."

"Anybody for another drink?" Thomas had sneaked up behind Sam and put his arm around her waist.

"Nope," someone said, "we're good for now."

"I need to talk to you," Thomas said toward Sam.

"Okay," Sam said, "do you want to go upstairs?"

Thomas nodded and they went upstairs to the hallway.

"What's this I hear about someone calling in to 911 anonymously and turning Clarence in?"

"Yah, not sure, don't know anything about it," Sam said.

"Don't you?" Thomas sounded mad. "It sounds like your work … and one of the neighbors thought it was you leaving the Tucci's yard. He just told me."

"All right," Sam said, "you caught me. Don't tell anyone but I'm the one that turned him in."

"I just keep asking myself why would you be hunting around in Clarence's garage?"

"I don't know," Sam said, "I just had my suspicions, that's all. So I went to take a look. Have you been talking to all my boys in the back or what?"

"No, I've just been talking to all our neighbors in the living room, why?"

"Just wondered. They aren't suppose to be talking about any of our cases … just wondered, that's all."

"Okay," Thomas relaxed and smiled. "Well you did a good thing … you know with Clarence ... and thanks for being honest about it." He kissed her lightly on the forehead twice.

"I have to go find Alex," Sam said as she turned and went down the stairs. She looked at the dancing couples in the front hall and realized that Thomas's golf clubs were like an obstacle that everyone had to dance around. Damn, she thought, should have put those away.

Sam saw Alex from across the room. She was surrounded by the neighbors, mostly men, who were all trying to get command of her attention. Alex looked gorgeous in a dark green sweater, her long red hair flowing over her shoulders.

Sam herself had her hair tied up and back, away from her face. Thomas had said earlier how beautiful she was, but Sam figured that Alex was the girl in the room that took any man's breath away. She looked like one of those famous old movie stars surrounded by her flock of love-struck groupies dripping off of her arms.

Alex was just finishing a story, the group listening intently, leaning in on her every word. She waived as Sam crossed the room toward her.

"And that's when I told him he had bird shit running down his back," Alex said. She stood smiling as the group released backward in one big, loud unanimous laugh.

"Ha that's funny, and I'll bet he went home and kicked himself for looking so stupid. You're amazing." one young man said. Sam thought his name was Cooper but she really wasn't sure.

"Why thank you," Alex said, "now if you'll give me a few minutes, I have to talk to our host." She grabbed Sam and led her away through the kitchen and sunroom into the backyard. There were only a couple of people standing in the semi-darkness near the back gate. Probably smoking, Sam thought, or smoking up.

"You look stunning," Sam said, "and by the way thanks for coming."

"Well thank you Sam," Alex said, "you look stunning yourself you know."

They hugged.

"So I have to let you know," Alex whispered, "MacKetchison is really pissed at everyone in the lab. He seems to think we're all on your personal crusade."

"What the hell?" Sam asked.

"Yah, he doesn't get it … he thinks we're all doing extra stuff but we are actually all working overtime on the serial case. I'm the only one that still knows anything about your stuff … and trust me, I won't be telling anyone else anything … so you don't have to worry."

"I know," Sam said, "I know I can trust you Alex, I'm not worried."

"So the good news is," Alex continued, "all those last samples you gave me worked fine. The glass worked great and now we have the DNA of the bastard who's been doing all this shit." She smiled and hugged Sam. "We'll catch the son of a bitch now."

"I hope so," Sam said, "I think it's starting to really get me down. I'm stressing out about everything and I can't even communicate properly with Thomas anymore. He just cornered me and asked why I was rummaging through the Tucci garage. It's getting rather unbearable."

They walked back inside and joined the group in the kitchen. Some of Sam's female neighbors had Robert and Frankie cornered and were drilling them for answers about the serial killer. Both were being polite by telling everyone around them that they couldn't discuss the ongoing case.

Sam rolled her eyes as she and Alex walked by. Both men looked flustered.

Sam and Alex went back to the living room and joined the group discussing Clarence and Vivian.

"But that's the thing," the neighbor Sam thought was named Cooper was saying, "the cops have never said who turned him in."

Another neighbor, Sid, piped up, "and nobody knows how much Vivian knows."

"How could she be living with him for all those years and not know." a woman named Shelby stated.

"Yah," said another neighbor named Erin. "I don't believe anyone could keep a secret like that from their sister, not when they're living together."

"What do you think Samantha?" Thomas asked Sam. He was leaning against the doorframe and Sam immediately decided he was looking incredibly sexy at that moment.

"Huh, well I don't know … people seem to lead double lives all the time … don't they?"

"Yup," said Erin. "You never know, she maybe just left the garage totally alone."

"Yah especially if he ordered her to," Cooper said.

"Either that or she knew everything and just let it go on anyway." Shelby said.

"I can't believe that," Sam said, "she just doesn't seem the type."

"Man, I just can't believe that we all lived that close to kiddy porn like that. I walk by that garage everyday to and from work." Erin said.

"You just can't trust anyone I guess," Thomas said.

"Well goes to show you, none of us will really ever know anyone entirely," Sam said, "not even when you're living with them or married to them." She stared at Thomas.

"I just keep wondering who found out and turned him in." Cooper said.

"Well it's like I told you before … I have my suspicions," Sid said.

Sam looked at Alex but she was already preoccupied with some of the other male neighbors.

chapter fifty six

Sam finished her third glass of wine. It's starting to really go down easily, she thought. She was standing with Melissa, Matt and Natalie. All four had been having a real heated discussion about the ethics of police and individual's right to privacy.

"I gotta get some more," she motioned to her glass. She was near the front hall where couples were still dancing to the tunes. She moved through the crowd back into the kitchen to find some more wine. The clock already read close to midnight.

"Surprise!" she yelled to no one in particular as she walked in to the kitchen. Then she laughed and waved to Robert. It wasn't quite as crowded now in the kitchen, it seemed everyone had gravitated toward the music.

"Hey," Robert said as he joined her at the counter. "You're having a good time partner."

"You bet," she said and smiled,"and are you having a good time?" She stumbled a little forward and put her arms up and around Roberts neck to brace herself.

"Oh yah I am Sam. Here come and sit down for a bit." He picked up her glass, held onto her arm and led her back to the sunroom.

Sam sat between Robert and Frankie. She looked down and realized her short, black dress had ridden up her thighs quite a bit. More than my colleagues should ever see, she thought as she lifted her ass and pushed her dress down her legs. When she looked up Frankie, Bruce, Phil, Tony and the two older cops were all looking at her legs. They all looked away awkwardly.

"Hey Sam," Frankie said, "where'd you go? Remember I was asking you earlier about your kitchen reno."

"Sorry, got sidetracked … I was just talking to a couple of friends of mine and telling them about the guy down the street with the garage full of kiddy porn."

"Yah," Phil said, "quite the hall, that one. That bastard is going away for a long time."

"So like I was asking you before," Frankie said, "it still smells like sawdust and paint in here, when did you get the reno done?"

Smell, smell, Sam thought. What smell? What … wait a minute … wait … Jennifer … her strong perfume … that's it … I can go around and smell everyone. I will never forget that strong cheap men's cologne.

Then I can catch the shit head that's fucked me up.

"The kitchen was finished just a month or two ago. By our main suspect … Barry." Sam laughed. "I gotta go use the can."

Sam started by sniffing near the men in the sunroom as she got up slowly pretending to go to the bathroom. All seemed a pleasant enough smelling group to Sam, some strong aftershave but nothing close to the cologne she was after.

She made her way into the kitchen and sniffed around another group of men. One of the ladies in the group handed her a tissue from Sam's Kleenex container on the counter. She nodded her thanks as she went into the front hall.

"Sam, come here!" Melissa waved. Her, Matt and Natalie were grooving on the dance floor. Matt looked like he was dancing with Thomas's clubs he kept touching them so much.

Sam joined them dancing. Dancing and laughing … she really liked her friends … they were so much fun … she knew then that she loved them all … and then the dance floor wobbled.

She was drunk.

The clock now read one forty and the crowd had started to thin out. Sam made her way around the living room sniffing each man while trying not to look too weird. Still no cheap, strong cologne.

She made her way back past the kitchen and sunroom and into the backyard. In the back alley by the gate, Sam wasn't sure but she thought she could make out Thomas talking to someone. She moved closer to take a better look but unfortunately forgot all about the small wire fence she had put down along the edge of the garden earlier in the spring. When her right foot got sloppy and caught the top of the wire and her left foot was in no position to catch her, she went down in between the row of cabbage and carrots.

"Oof," was all she said as she hit the ground. But fuck, fuck, fuck was all she thought. Fucking fence! God I better not have fucked my Jenny Qui's, she thought, they're my favorite shoes! And my dress! Fuck.

"Are you okay Sam?" Thomas asked as he reached for her.

She stood up slowly, head beginning to swirl. She held tight to Thomas.

"Who were you talking to?" she asked.

"Oh that," Thomas said, "it was nothing … just work."

She was blonde and Sam thought she looked beautiful. She had just caught a really quick glimpse as she went down so she couldn't be sure. Who was the woman? Was that someone Thomas had to hide?

"Well why didn't you invite her in?" Sam brushed off the dirt from her dress.

"She was in a hurry Sam, come on let's get you inside." He took her by the arm and started to lead her inside.

She stopped "Well, you should have introduced me …"

"Sam the first I knew you were back here was when I saw you on the ground."

"Yah well …"

"Come on Mrs Dahill," he said as he pushed her inside.

He parked her in the kitchen at the counter talking to Jennifer.

Sam was still enjoying herself when most of her guests had gone. The clock now read two thirty. She had finished another couple of glasses. She was bouncing in and out of a conversation with neighbors Jennifer and Shelby, but mostly she completely lost track of what they were talking about. She started to worry about Thomas and his mysterious blonde.

Was that part of his double life? She let her mind wander. Was he hiding the mystery woman in the back hoping Sam wouldn't see her so Sam would never know her husband had two wives? What could she do? She would have to confront him. Did the other woman know?

"Sam, Sam," Thomas said, "wake up Sam." He put his arm around her and helped her up. "Come on, I'll put you to bed honey." All their house guests seemed to be gone.

Sam half walked and was half dragged upstairs and into bed. Thomas removed her shoes and dress but left her underwear on and laid her out on their bed under the covers.

"You'll live honey," he said, "I'll sleep downstairs on the couch."

"Okay honey bunny," Sam said, "I love you … you know … and who was that woman?" She pulled the covers up.

"And I'm sorry," she said, "for not telling you everything about my secret lover … his hands … I love those hands … I just wish … I … I …"

But Thomas was already downstairs cleaning up.

chapter fifty seven

Sam and Robert were in the boardroom again. Surrounded by towers of file folders and sticky notes everywhere. Sunday morning was quiet at the precinct. Sam and Robert had both decided to meet and go over some of the case that morning.

Sam was still staring at a note she found Saturday afternoon. Thomas had left it for her after their party on Friday night. All it stated was that he was called away on an emergency for a few days and had to leave early Saturday morning. Sam hadn't even had a chance to see him or say goodbye. She had overslept his departure. Hell, she had overslept most of Saturday, she realized. She missed Thomas already.

It was that woman, Sam thought, he had left because of her. Sam had to find out who she was and what part she played in Thomas's life.

"Well I just don't see how we are going to ever find this guy if we can't get any evidence." Sam said.

"I know," Robert said, "but the guy is really good. He just doesn't leave anything behind."

"It's getting really frustrating."

"It's been a couple of months now and we are still clueless, damn right it's frustrating. The computer lead flamed out. The surveillance tapes didn't amount to anything … damn."

"The only suspect and we can't pin anything on him." Sam said.

"And we've followed Barry around and discovered squat."

"Is the tailing detail still on him?"

"Nope," Robert said. "Don't think so, upper said we didn't have the budget to go more than a week or two."

"Too bad, he may have led us somewhere eventually."

"And to make things worse," Robert said, "Ron just told me that the Mayor is so pissed with us, he doesn't want any of our contract negotiations to go through."

"Great," Sam said. "Just what we need. That will really piss everyone off when they find that out."

"Hey Sam, what about setting a trap up for this asshole?"

"A trap?" asked Sam. "Like what? How?"

"I don't know … but there has to be something. Maybe we could just let it be known around town about a couple of women being available and then plant a couple in key locations ... I don't know ..."

"I think it's stretching it a little too far, don't you think ... we wouldn't be able to cover the entire city."

"Yah," Robert said, "you're probably right ... stupid idea."

"Hey what about faking some evidence?" Sam asked.

"What do you mean?"

"Well, maybe we could flush him out if we came out with a statement to the press. We could say we have new evidence linking Barry to the last murder or one of the first murders or something."

"And?"

"Well," continued Sam, "maybe that would be enough for Barry to make a move and make a mistake. Or if it isn't Barry, maybe someone else would come out of the woodwork and make a mistake."

"Okay let me think about it and we'll figure something out," Robert said, "and just so no one can get into serious trouble, let's not tell anyone else what we're thinking of doing okay?"

"I agree," Sam said, "we can't trust anyone ..."

Robert gave her a quizzical look.

chapter fifty eight

Sam got into work very early Monday morning hoping she could rummage through the desks of Tony and Frankie before anyone else arrived at the precinct.

Quick grab of something personal, she thought, what could go wrong?

The early morning sun was cutting through the bright room at an odd angle, too early for most to ever see. Sam took off her coat and shoes and made her way over to Tony's desk. The room smelled of dust, burnt coffee and donuts.

Tony was another messy and unorganized cop. What else is new, Sam thought as she shuffled through the stack of papers on Tony's desk.

She picked the cheap drawer lock and slid his main drawer open. Pens and paper and not much else. She checked under the papers but couldn't find anything of use.

She looked at the photo of Tony and his ex-girlfriend and wondered what Tony would be like to live with. A bit larger than life usually, Tony could be loud and kind of obnoxious, But Sam still liked him. He just seemed to be compensating for something, maybe a lack of self-esteem? Sam thought.

Tony was a Hispanic American and a bit older than Sam with a head full of deep black hair. Apparently his hair had been black since he was a young man, but Sam couldn't be sure. She always wondered if he used any product, but she never dared ask him. Not exactly handsome, but definitely not on the ugly side either. He looked just a little plain, Sam thought, maybe like a neighbor that you've never really noticed living on your street.

She sat daydreaming of Tony running his hands over her naked body. What would it be like, she wondered, if he was the one who was showing you the orgasmic secrets of your body?

She tried the right side drawer. Beside a small stack of books and a spare box of ammo, Sam saw what she needed. Tony's hairbrush was covered in black hair. She poked through and found a couple of hairs with the follicles still attached. She placed the hairs into an envelope marked 10) Tony Hernandes.

And now on to the other one, she thought, closing up Tony's desk drawers and moving over to Frankie's area.

Frankie was an entirely different type of policeman. Desk and surrounding area well thought out and tidy. Everything placed on shelves and in neat boxes. Methodical with his workspace and Sam knew that was how he liked to run his investigations as well. She wondered what it was like between the two partners. Which one was the person who compromised and let the other have their way? Or did they both compromise like a long term marriage?

Frankie was an Asian American with a really funny sense of humor. He was always playing jokes on the group and thought everything in scales of laughter. Sam sat at his desk and tried to think about her secret lover. Frankie? Really? She couldn't really think of him in any kind of sexual way. Wouldn't he be in giggling fits most of the time, not the seriousness of those hands caressing her in all the proper places.

She picked the lock and opened the main top drawer. Inside she shuffled a few things around and peeked under a stack of forms. There was a fingernail file laying on the bottom of the drawer. She picked it up and was just placing it into an envelope marked 11) Frankie Shapiro when she heard a loud voice behind her. Fuck.

"What the fuck are you doing Dahill?" It was Tony.

"I'm … a … just … ah …" Holy fuck, think girl think! Her mind went blank. Fuck … she hadn't even heard anyone come in.

"Well, what the hell are you doing?" He leaned over Sam and looked closely at the envelope.

"I'm just looking … around," she said.

"What the fuck! Have you gone fucking nuts? Have you lost your fucking mind?" Tony was pissed and yelling.

"No," she said as she turned and stood, "relax Tony."

"You think one of us is the serial killer?" Asked Frankie.

"Well fuck you …" Tony yelled, "what, your probably brown nosing, collecting everyone's DNA for Ron are you? He put you up to this didn't he?"

"No," Sam said, "its not like that … come on guys."

"Well what is it then?" Frankie asked.

"I don't think either of you guys … hell none of us is the serial killer. Look the lab just wanted some base DNA samples that they could use to compare crime scene DNA to," she lied.

"Yah right, let them get their own samples," Tony said, "now give Frankie back his nail file."

Sam handed the envelope to Frankie and apologized. She walked back to her desk and sat down, putting her head in her hands. I really fucked that one up, she thought. Fuck.

She felt frustrated and stupid and all she could think was that she wished she had left for the office even earlier that morning.

Robert appeared with coffee and fresh biscuits and a large smile. That cheered Sam up and she soon forgot all about Tony and Frankie.

In the afternoon Robert received a call from the Organized Crime Task Force. They needed help. He told Sam to be prepared to go undercover Thursday night.

chapter fifty nine

Sam walked into the squad room Thursday night and was immediately swept up by a hurricane of cat whistles. Almost every police constable and detective turned and whistled in her direction.

She was wearing a short, red sequined dress with her high strapped Jenny Qui shoes, disheveled hair and heavy makeup. Not quite her hooker impersonation, but close. She was dressed as the sleaze next door who likes to party. She was off to the Sound Shelter Club downtown to follow some scum suspect around for the night.

And when she walked into the room she was steaming mad at her Captain for making her get dressed like a sleazy clubber to go undercover. Why couldn't she just go in as a normal person? She had asked her commander earlier but he had just come up with some excuse of being available if the suspect got interested. What the fuck? Was she expected to fuck the guy if he liked her look? Sorry but that's not in my job description, she thought.

She answered the whistles by giving all the guys her middle finger, straight and upright and in front of her glaring eyes as she slowly walked across the room being careful in her heels.

After the whistling died down, she heard a couple of the guys yell out.

"Wow you're really hot Dahill!"

"Holy shit Dahill, where you hiding your gun?" Laughter.

She flushed. She dropped her head slightly and walked over to her desk.

"Hey kiddo," Robert said, "you look really nice."

"Yah right," was all she could get out as she sat down. She quickly turned in to her desk to cover her legs. It seemed that her skirt didn't cover much even pulled down. Fuck she thought, if she leaned forward at all, she would be able to see her own thong. Oh my God, she thought, how am I ever going to pull this off? I can't sit down … I won't be able sit down anywhere else … I won't.

"Very different look for you though, I got to admit."

"Well don't get used to it," she said. "I am not into prancing around here like a whore."

She had studied herself earlier in the bathroom mirror after she had changed and ruffled her hair and caked on her make up. She wasn't used to the look. It was a strain to recognize herself. She thought she looked kind of silly, like a young girl dressing up in her mommy's grown-up clothes. Her mommy's come over here and fuck me hard outfit. She didn't belong in this type of club, did she?

When she had looked closely at her dress she realized how glad she was that she had put on her thong underneath. You could see every line, every shape, she couldn't have gotten away with her usual panties. It was either that or go commando, no underwear at all. But she had never done that before in her life. She didn't dare.

Robert smiled. "So when are we leaving?"

Sam took her smaller back-up gun out from her desk drawer and put it carefully in her small handbag.

"We can't get there too early," Sam said, "we have to blend in and no one arrives there before about eleven thirty or midnight."

"Okay we'll shoot for eleven forty five."

chapter sixty

Sam walked into the nightclub and let her eyes adjust to the contrast of dark corners and bright flashing lights near the bars and dance floor. The smell of booze and young hopeful sex filled the air.

House music and big beats bounced around the room filling the air with an electric vibration that enveloped Sam's mind. She tried to blend in as she checked her hidden microphone and earpiece.

"What did you say?" she said into the mike, "I can't hear a fucking thing in here … it's deafening."

"I asked if you were going to be … …. …?" one of the guys asked, she thought it sounded like Frankie or Bruce.

"My what?" she asked.

"Your booty … your big ass … your sweet …" the voice said.

"Fuck you," she said.

"Okay that's enough everybody," Robert said. "Just determine if our guy is in there Sam, Okay? That's the first step. We'll stand by until confirmation."

"Will do," she said and walked over to the VIP section trying to look as sexy as she could think of.

It was a bit quieter in the back as Sam found the VIP section. There were two large suits standing guard in front of one of the areas but Sam couldn't see who was behind. She decided to try to walk by casually as if going somewhere further along. Out of the side of her sight, she saw someone disappear behind the back curtain but it was too quick for her to see who it was.

"Hey sugar," the suit on the left said, "you into some fun?"

"Maybe," Sam said.

He reached out and grasped her left elbow firmly. "The boss likes to have fun." He steered her into the table area. In the center of the low swooping couch sat Antonio Briggs, the notorious drug lord. The supposed head of the West Side. He was flanked by two ladies on each side. It surprised Sam that they all looked close to her age and not a lot younger.

"Hey baby what's your name," Antonio asked.

"Amanda," Sam said.

"Well sit down here Amanda and lets party," he said pushing the girls down the bench.

What the hell have I gotten myself into? Sam thought. She sat down and crossed her legs to keep her thong to herself.

Antonio waved at the waiter who appeared suddenly and placed a drink in front of Sam.

"Here's to beautiful women," Antonio picked up his glass and motioned to Sam, "may they always be horny." He smiled at Sam.

"Right," said Sam. She took a sip. Some sort of raspberry martini. Not bad, she thought, not bad.

She looked around as she held up her glass. The two closest women were wearing short dresses like her, but the other two on both ends were in pantsuits and looked like they were dressed more for security. Maybe more bodyguards? Sam thought.

The two in the short dresses leaned over and started to fondle Antonio, stroking his chest and hair. One girl was almost laying on top of Sam in order to reach Antonio but the girl didn't seem to notice or care.

It didn't take Sam very long to feel the effects of the drink. As the girls laughed and talked and fondled, she felt as though she was slipping below the table. Whatever drug that had been put in her drink, was really quick, she thought. She started to lose control of her limbs.

Antonio reached over to her and pulled her up slightly on the seat. He leaned over and said something to the girl by Sam's side who then rolled over Sam again and lay almost completely on top of her. The girl laughed.

Sam tried to speak. Say something! she said to herself. Come on bitch, yell into the mike! Do something! But she couldn't move. If the girl or anyone else had cared to look at Sam then, they would have seen the fear rise up in her eyes. But still no movement.

Oh my God, Sam thought. What is happening? I can't do anything. Help Robert, help.

Antonio said something to the group and they all stood up together. She could feel the ladies pick her up and start to carry her out the back. She was carried upright as though walking by the two in the pantsuits, feet dragging behind. As they reached the back hallway, Antonio padded her down and found the tiny wire and mike. He ripped the mike off her body and threw it back into the nightclub. Then he reached toward her earpiece. He hesitated and then laughed.

"No," he said, "we'll let you hear them panic when they can't find you."

When they reached the alley, they turned a corner and threw Sam into the back of a limo that sat idling, driver behind the wheel.

Antonio climbed into the limo along with all four girls and one of the suits. Sam could see the other suit climb in front beside the driver. She could watch everything but couldn't move, couldn't speak. She was sitting crumpled on the floor with her legs sprawled out in from of her, her dress hiked up around her waist and her black thong fully visible to everyone. Antonio pushed his foot between her legs and against her vagina with the toe of his shoe. Her light, flimsy thong was no protection from his hard leather.

The limo pulled away as tears started down both of Sam's cheeks. Antonio slapped Sam hard once across the face. Her head snapped to the side violently. He reached down and turned her head back and propped it upright so she could see him as he yelled at her.

"Fucking Cunt," Antonio yelled. "Fucking cop cunt. Did you think we didn't spot you the moment you walked in? Stupid bitch!"

The limo stopped and another male climbed in over Sam and sat down between the ladies. It was fucking Teddy Knight. A low level drug dealer that worked the downtown area. Sam had busted him a few times years ago when she was still walking the beat. So that's how she had been made so quickly. Shit, they hadn't thought of that.

Teddy smiled, "Teddy never forgets a face bitch."

The limo started up again as Antonio continued, "and such a fucking fine face too." He shook his head. "What a waste of such fine pussy."

He pushed on her crotch again. She felt so helpless and scared. He could split her wide open and she couldn't do anything about it.

Fear … panic … terror …

"Sam, Sam, where are you?" Sam could hear Robert's voice in her ear.

I am going to die now, she thought. Poor Robert will never forgive himself for letting her die. And poor Thomas, he won't ever know what happened to his wife. He won't ever know his real wife. The wife who has been terrorized all this time and couldn't tell anyone. The wife that loves him so deeply but never gets the chance to show him, doesn't know how. Her eyes welled up with tears so badly she could barely see.

"We are going to have so much fun raping you bitch," Antonio laughed. He leaned over Sam and spoke quietly into her ear. "You're going to hear all your comrades calling for you as we rape you slowly one by one." He slid his hand down her dress to her crotch and touched her thong. He slid his hand under her thong and massaged her clit with his index and middle finger.

Stop that you fucking asshole! Sam yelled inside. Fuck! Don't you dare touch me! But only silence came out of her. She watched as Antonio licked his lips.

"Sam, Sam, come in Sam. Is everything okay?" she could hear Robert again.

"Ah she's probably enjoying herself too much," Frankie said.

"Well I don't know," Robert said, "maybe we should send somebody inside. Phil go see how she is doing."

"Okay, will do," Phil answered.

Antonio pulled his hand away, leaned back and laughed along with Teddy and the girls. He put his fingers up to his nose and sniffed … he smiled and blew Sam a kiss.

The car continued to sway and swerve as it made it's way down the road.

chapter sixty one

Sam sat and waited for her death. She decided to just let it come. She knew she wouldn't enjoy being raped numerous times but she decided that there was nothing she could do about it. At least the physical feelings of her body was gone, she just felt numb. Her brain wasn't receiving anything physical anymore. Get it over with, you fuck head, she thought looking at Antonio.

She just hoped she would die with what dignity she had left. She just hoped they didn't start sticking their dicks down her throat or in her ass while raping her with anything other than their penises. She didn't like reading about those kinds of cases when they happened. She had helped arrest a couple of teenagers who had done that to a poor girl back a few years. They used a few different household items to rape her, a broom handle, a beer bottle and the handle from a hammer, she remembered. The girl had slowly bled to death inside while they continued to torture her over and over. It was horrible.

And Sam thought of the serial killer as well. This monster who killed his victims in the most degrading way he could possibly think of. Someone who must really hate women. How could someone hate anyone that much that you could perform such acts to another human being? Choking a helpless female by shoving nylons down her throat with his penis. He made Briggs look like an amateur, and yet there she was, stuck with the amateur, waiting to die.

How could I let myself get into this? Sam thought. Some big tough cop now huh. Can't even take care of myself. Go undercover and ten minutes later drugged and lined up as the ultimate gang bang and raping prize. Step right up ladies and gentlemen and fuck the paralyzed cop. Fuck her, kick her, beat her, do anything you want to her, she can't move.

Sam couldn't even close her eyes but her mind wandered in spite of that. Thomas, oh Thomas, please save me, she thought. Please. Where are you Thomas? She thought of the stranger's gentle hands moving over her body. The confidence of the motion, knowing just what she needed to turn her on so. The beautiful hands that were so gentle and always felt so wonderful. Maybe they could save her ...

Antonio kicked her in the crotch again, only this time quite hard. She felt nothing, just watched.

And the limo suddenly stopped throwing all of its occupants forward.

"Hey," yelled Briggs just as all the doors were ripped open.

"Samantha!" Robert yelled as Briggs lunged. Robert blocked him and punched him twice quickly in the face. Briggs went down hard on the floor beside Sam.

A flood of relief hit Sam as she sat wanting to kick Briggs in the head herself. She waited for Robert to pick her up off the floor and carry her out of the car.

"I'm so sorry partner," Robert said, "we never for a moment thought you would be made so quickly." He carried her over to his car and placed her in the passenger seat. The others were being pulled out of the limo by a few detectives, others stood back covering the group with their Glocks.

"Call an ambulance Phil," Robert yelled. "Be right back Sam."

Sam watched as Robert grabbed Antonio's feet and pulled him straight out of the vehicle and onto the ground. Antonio's shoulders and head flopped over the door frame and smacked down onto the pavement. Robert rolled him over and tied his hands together with two twist ties. Then he walked back and sat down in the driver's seat beside Sam leaving both doors open.

"Shit I'm sorry kid. I never thought anything like this would happen," Robert said. "We tracked your earpiece. Both your mike and earpiece have GPS just in case … lucky that."

Sam thought Robert seemed so cute at that moment, he was so serious and concerned. Her shock made her think only one thought, how glad she had worn a thong at least instead of going commando. Robert already saw more skin than she wanted her partner to ever see. If she had been commando, she thought, he would have easily then been able to swear that yes, she was a natural brunette. She wondered if anyone else saw her black thong as well. She really wished she had been wearing a pair of her regular panties or better yet, a pair of her big white grannie panties. Damn.

Sam was just starting to feel like her body could respond to movement again as they sat and waited for the ambulance to come.

chapter sixty two

The sun was coming up when the affects of the drug finally wore off. Sam and Robert were sitting on the back bumper of the ambulance, Robert's arm around Sam's shoulders.

"Thanks Robert," Sam said, "for staying with me all this time."

"Hey no prob kid," he said, "least I could do after putting you in so much danger. Damn we really screwed up."

"Well at least you got Antonio Briggs for something, kidnapping no less."

"Yup, the bastard … wished I could of killed him," he said.

"Me too," said Sam.

"And I can't believe how quick that drug took effect."

"I know," Sam shook her head, "I had only taken a couple of sips."

"We'll have to get it analyzed and see what it is."

"God I sure hope that stuff doesn't start hitting the streets," she said.

"Now go home and tell Thomas what happened and crawl into a nice warm bath or something."

"No way!" she said quickly. "You have to promise me that you won't tell Thomas anything ... that you will never tell him what happened ... I have to be able to take care of myself ... he can never know that sometimes I can't."

"Come on Sam, you have to let him know."

"No," she said, "he would make me quit my job ... he'd never let me stay a cop. And I'm sure you know by now, I can't do anything else, I'd never last ... I was made for this."

They drove back to the precinct so Sam could retrieve her car. Robert was worried that she shouldn't be driving, but Sam assured him she was fine. She removed her shoes and tossed them onto the passenger seat. Her expensive Jenny Qui's, ripped at the toe and scuffed all up both sides. Handbag and gun gone. Fuck.

When she got home, Thomas was sitting at the kitchen table nursing a cup of coffee. He turned as she walked in.

"My God," he jumped up from his seat. "What the fuck happened?" He ran over to Sam and put his arms around her and hugged tightly.

"Ouch," she said.

"Sorry, here come and sit down." He guided her to the couch and they both sat down, his arm around her shoulders. He pulled her close and cuddled her head.

"Just a fight at work that's all," she said. "We were out of uniform, trying to locate a suspect and things just got out of hand."

"But you're okay?" he asked concerned.

"Yes I'll be fine, no harm done," she lied.

She sat quietly in Thomas's arms for a moment and then a wave of held emotion hit her hard. Her eyes teared up and she began to cry.

"Oh Sam," Thomas said, "I wish I could always protect you …"

If only you could, Sam thought, if only you could.

chapter sixty three

The call came in early Sunday morning. Another body was found. Sam woke up alone in her bed. Thomas was in Washington again just for a couple of nights.

As Sam got into her car a tinge of familiarity pushed through the back of her brain. Something is wrong … wait … what … holy fuck! It was Natalie's address! Sam's heart leapt and began to pump quicker. She could barely breath as she drove to the apartment. Her blood felt like it was going to burst through her chest and her head.

Poor Nat, Sam thought, what could be wrong? Focus bitch … you ran a red light!

She pulled up and ran in past the officers and the Medical Examiner. Sam stopped at the doorway of Natalie's bedroom. Natalie was posed like the others. Naked and on her knees by her bed. Hands tied behind her back, eyes hidden behind a mask, mouth forced open with a gag.

Sam slumped down against the doorframe as Robert stood up from behind the body.

"Sam," he said as he walked toward her. He pulled her up and walked her back into the kitchen. "Here sit," he steered her toward a chair.

What the fuck happened? What happened to Nat? What's going on? Sam was blank. Her mind was numb … everything was blurry. Her eyes pooled up.

"Just sit here Sam," Robert said holding her shoulders. "Don't do anything okay?" He turned and went back into the bedroom.

I was just talking to Nat a few days ago, Sam thought, we danced together … she was so happy … she talked about starting a new job and meeting a new guy … what was happening … poor Nat …

"Samantha?" it was Natalie's mother, Debbie. She sat down beside Sam and they both leaned together and hugged. Both were openly crying.

Sam sat hugging Debby for what seemed like a long time. Neither woman felt like pulling away. Neither had anywhere to go.

They finally pulled back and looked at each other. Tears still streaming down their faces.

"Oh Samantha," Debbie said, "I don't know what happened. I came over early to pick Natalie up, we were going to go to the market. I walked in … and …"

"It's okay Debbie," Sam said. "Try not to think about it." She hugged Debbie again.

Sam stood up and walked over to the sink. She ran some cold water and splashed her face. She felt she had to get her shit together. She pulled a glass from the cupboard and filled it from the tap.

"I have to go help with the investigation," she said. "Don't move, just sit." She placed the glass of water in front of Debbie.

Sam returned to the bedroom. Robert was talking with the Medical Examiner, more or less trying to determine time of death.

I can do this, Sam thought, I need to do this ... for Nat's sake ... I need to help catch this bastard and stop all this madness. She stood over the body. Poor Nat ... no stop ... stop thinking of this as a friend ... be cold and get through this.

"Are you okay?" Robert asked. "I'm really sorry Sam ... you know I can call someone else in ..."

"I'll be fine," Sam said, "I want to do this ... I need to do this."

"Alright, here's what we have so far. Natalie Warner, aged 28, mother Debbie, finds her at approximately seven thirty am.

Her whereabouts last night so far unknown and yet to be determined."

"Please tell me something I don't already know."

"Ya well I'm getting to that," Robert said.

"Did you know that she just filed a police report yesterday. Her apartment, this apartment, was broken into two nights ago."

So that's why there were three messages from Natalie on my voicemail yesterday, Sam thought. I got them so late, I was going to call today. Fuck.

"Fuck," Sam said, "I should have called her last night ... She left three messages on my voicemail. I maybe could have stopped ...."

"This isn't your fault Sam," Robert said. "You can't think like that."

If only I had called, she thought. It was probably around eleven thirty ... I could have called. I should have called.

"What time was death? Sam asked.

"Examiner figures around two thirty to three thirty am or so. And it looks like she put up a bit of a struggle Sam."

"Oh why is that?"

"Take a look at this," Robert was pointing down toward Natalie's crotch below her naked belly, her knees spread wide.

"Sorry partner," he bent down and pointed between Natalie's bare legs. "See all the hair on the floor, looks like it was ripped from her head, she was probably struggling. Our killer's never had to do that before."

Sam looked around the room. It felt weird being this close to the victim. She didn't feel comfortable, she felt like she shouldn't be there, she was invading a close friend's personal space. There were a couple of photos of family hanging on the wall and one photo sitting on the bureau of the whole gang.

Sam walked over to the photo and looked closer. It showed the smiling faces of Sam and Thomas, Natalie, Melissa and Matt, and a few other old friends around a smoldering campfire. The photo was taken with Natalie's camera on the self-timer, Sam remembered. Two summers ago when they all arranged to go camping in the hills for the long weekend. It was such a blast, Sam thought back to how they had hiked each day, all day long, and then sat around the campfire drinking and telling funny stories each night. On the second morning

Natalie had them all gather around while she propped up the camera and put on the self timer. For all time, Sam remembered that was what Nat had said at the time. For all time, so they could remember the fun and friendship of that moment forever.

Tears started down Sam's cheeks as she turned away.

chapter sixty four

The ride back to the precinct was quiet and heavy. Robert had insisted that Sam ride with him and leave her car at Natalie's for now. He told her she was in no shape to drive.

Sunday morning traffic was relatively light, Robert took the freeway part way. Most of the cars, even on the freeway, seemed to be making their way slowly and casually to places like the markets or possibly church. No one in a hurry, not like a weekday when everyone drives insanely like their lives depend on getting to the office early.

Sam stared out the passenger window and let Chicago float by. No reaction necessary, I don't need to move, thought Sam. Just sit, let the world pass by, nothing matters, she is not needed.

Her mind wandered. One of my best friends is now gone and I never get to hear her laugh again. Life is too short and cheap. Life is horribly unforgiving, no responsibility. You live and love people and then a monster comes along and takes everyone away. What a waste ... what a waste of a beautiful life ... poor Nat ...

When they walked into the precinct, they were immediately summoned into Ron's office. Ron was dressed casually behind his desk. Called in early on a Sunday, caught in sweats and hoody.

"I understand you knew the victim pretty well," Ron said.

"Yes, she was a close friend," Sam replied.

"Well, I'm sorry for your loss Sam. You're too close to this case now for you to stay investigating it. I'll have to put Phil and Bruce on it."

"No sir, please," Sam said, "I'll be fine, I'll be professional, I won't jeopardize the investigation in any way. I have to do this, I was close to her … please for Natalie's sake."

Now she really wanted to stay on this case. Her earlier hesitations and fears wanting to be pulled off the case had all evaporated. She wanted to catch this asshole shit head … more than anything … to avenge Nat's death …

"Well I want you watching her closely," Ron stood up and pointed to Robert, "at the first sign of any problems and I want you dumping her off this case and bringing her in. I'm leaving you responsible. Got that?"

"You bet," Robert said.

"Now whats your plan to find this guy?" Ron asked.

"First off," Robert said, "we were going to be spending the day at the coroner's to see if there was anything left at the scene."

"Then we'll canvass the neighbors and see if anyone saw anything," Sam said.

"Well for starters why don't you two go bring in your main suspect Barry again. Maybe this time you can get him to confess to this latest murder," Ron said.

"Thanks Ron," Sam said as they stood to go.

"And hey," Ron sat back down, "how's the viewing going of the surveillance tape? Got anything yet out of all that footage?"

"Not yet," Sam said, "but we'll let you know when we do."

Sam went to her desk and sat without even removing her coat. Robert picked up the phone and started trying to track down Barry.

How could they come up with any leads to pin down Barry, Sam thought, when they couldn't even figure out any kind of a connection between the victims. They had nothing in common. The only reason all the ladies were known to the police was because they had either filed complaints against someone or filled out police reports for robberies or such. And now with Nat gone, Sam felt like she had to use her intimate knowledge of her friend to be able to make any kind of connection.

I should be able to figure this out, she reasoned. I know what Nat was into, her work, her nightlife, and all of her other friends. What was it she said about her new job? Something about the people she worked with. She was now doing research for some big firm. What was the name of the company? Some pharmaceutical company downtown, wasn't it? And wait, wasn't there something else she told us at the party? What was it?

Sam sat still and tried to let her mind wander back to the night of the party.

Okay got it, she thought, Nat mentioned it, she met someone new. She had been out on a couple of dates … what was his name … what did she tell me? Fuck, I'm always so bad with names.

"Barry's disappeared again," Robert said as he hung up the phone, "gone underground … hasn't been seen anywhere."

"Shit," Sam stood and moved toward the boardroom, "let's see if we can figure out where he's hiding this time."

They moved to the boardroom but the stacks of files seemed overwhelming to Sam.

"Have you thought over what I said about sending out a fake press release?" Sam asked.

"Yah," Robert said, "a little ... what were you thinking?"

They drew out a plan. They typed up a fake statement letter and printed out two copies. They put one on Phil's desk in the squad room when he and Bruce were out, and the other one in Ron's mail slot. That way, they figured, with multiple copies it would look more official.

The letter went into detail how the two lead investigators had reviewed the surveillance tapes from the latest killing and had a pretty good idea of what the real killer looked like. It was only a matter of time before he would be identified. Of course it was ridiculous, they both knew already that the surveillance tapes probably would never reveal anything at the crime scene, but they figured that way they could keep it rather vague and not get caught in a completely fictitious lie and be disciplined in any way. Plus no one in the public would probably ever be able to find out who the lead investigators were anyway. Barry may have been able to guess but even he didn't really know that.

"And as soon as we get the word out, we just have to sit back and let Barry make his move. He'll probably take off and run," Robert said.

"But at least he'll surface," Sam said.

"And remember to protect everyone, we can't tell anyone anything about it. Got it?"

chapter sixty five

Sam and Robert had parked at the front and took the stairs down to the lab. Alex had called Sam and told her they had found something.

The lab was full, technicians everywhere, MacKetchison busy bossing them from the doorway to his office.

"So what's with the find?" Robert asked Alex as they entered the lab.

"Come and take a look at this," Alex said. "We found something interesting about the hairs you found at the scene."

"So you processed them already?" Sam asked.

"We aim to please," Alex smiled, "I jumped on them as soon as I got them a couple of hours ago."

She pointed to the two screens on the counter.

"All these hairs match the victim's hair," she said looking at the left screen, "but take a look at these two." She pointed to the screen on the right.

"They're different?" Robert asked.

"Yup," Alex said, "they sure are. They were in amongst the pile of hair, same general dark color and only slightly shorter so the murderer probably didn't even notice them."

"So you can maybe pull DNA from them?" Robert asked.

"But I thought you needed follicles attached to the hair to be able to get DNA off of them?" asked Sam.

"That's right Sam," Alex said, "but aren't we the luckiest bitches in the world. Sorry Robert. One of the hairs had the follicle attached."

"No fucking way!" Sam said.

"Wow," Robert said, "we might actually be able to prove Barry did it."

All three smiled as they thought of the consequences.

Sam was thinking of Natalie. Thanks Nat, she said to herself, you may have just broken the case wide open.

"Let's go catch the son of a bitch," Robert said as he walked out of the lab.

"I need to talk with you," Alex whispered.

"Okay call me later and we can get together okay?" Sam said. She turned and followed Robert out.

chapter sixty six

First stop they tried Barry's house but he wasn't to be found. None of his neighbors had seen him all day. Next stop they decided was the renovated place where they found Barry the first time. They weren't really expecting him to be there, but they thought they had better try anyway.

"You never know," Robert said, "probably stranger things have happened."

"And there has been dumber criminals than that," Sam said.

But Barry wasn't there either. They looked all around, inside and out. It didn't look like anyone had been there for a week or two.

They moved to the next location. The mother's long term care facility. They found the pretty nurse Jennifer Delatte and questioned her but she hadn't seen Barry for a number of days.

They drove downtown and parked. They sat in the parking lot looking out over the lake. The sun had turned the water into a sparkling carpet of jewels. People were out everywhere enjoying a sunny Sunday afternoon, walking up and down the walkway and sunbathing on the beach.

"We have to start to think like this guy," Robert said.

"Well I'm sorry but I can't," Sam said. She climbed out of the car. "Let's go get an ice cream."

"I don't mean the killing part Sam," Robert said as he got out of the car, "I just mean where would he hide, that kind of thing."

"Well," Sam said, "we've issued another BOLO so I doubt he's going to get very far once he does surface … you know after seeing the news."

"You mean after hearing about our fake surveillance sighting."

She ordered a Nutty Crunch ice cream cone and Robert tried a coconut cream bar.

"Yah, I know you don't like it very much but what else can we do … you know to find him?"

They walked along by the beach, dripping and licking. It was hot and both of them had taken their jackets off and thrown them over their arms. Without thinking, they had both attached their badges to their belts so the public wouldn't panic when they saw the shoulder holsters and Glocks. Sam started to feel a bit more human after the horrible morning with Natalie.

It was good therapy for Sam to watch the people. There were families with babies and toddlers and kids of many different ages. Each busy with their family duties tending to one another. Sam felt a bit isolated from everyone but at least a little necessary. A protector of such. Her and her badge and gun. Protecting the people … but from what … she couldn't even protect herself in her own bedroom. Fuck, she thought, I want Barry and I want to kill him.

They arrived back at Robert's car.

"I'll drop you off at your car and we can meet back at the station," he said.

When they reached Natalie's apartment and pulled up to her car, Sam had a thought.

"What if we never find Barry?" she asked.

"Don't worry," Robert said, "assholes like him always turn up."

She was about to get into her car when she noticed someone was still inside Natalie's apartment. She ducked under the crime tape and entered the apartment.

"Hi Bill," she said. Bill Lambert, chief of forensics field technicians was still wandering around the empty bedroom.

"Hello Samantha," he said. He was always such a sullen type of man. The work I guess, Sam thought.

"Hey do you think after you are done here today that I could take that photo," Sam pointed to the photo of her, Natalie and the camping group on the bureau.

"You can take it now," he said, "I'm done with it."

And so she did.

chapter sixty seven

Sam beat Robert back to the station. He made some excuse about stopping for dry cleaning, but Sam knew it was because he drove like a grandmother.

They were in the boardroom going through leads when the call came in. Barry had been spotted at a truck stop south on I55 toward St. Louis.

"Let's go partner," Robert said as he hung up the phone. "Your car or mine?"

"Let's take yours," she said, "my air conditioning hasn't been working very well lately."

They grabbed their coats and found Robert's car at the far end of the parking lot. Robert promised that once they hit the highway, he would speed up.

It took them close to forty five minutes down the 55 to find the stop long before Pontiac. They talked to all the waitresses and canvassed the patrons, showing Barry's picture to everyone they could find. When they finally tracked down one of the resident truck mechanics, they found what they were looking for. He had remembered a guy catching a ride with the driver of a black Willis truck heading south a few hours earlier. But he didn't get a very good look at him so he couldn't be sure.

Sam and Robert decided to take the chance and continued down the highway.

"So," Sam said, "have you ever thought what you'd do if you weren't a cop?"

"Nope," Robert said. "I can't imagine myself doing anything else. How about you?"

"I don't know," she leaned back and closed her eyes, "I've thought about it of course, but nothing's really come to mind. I don't think I could do anything else, it just wouldn't feel right. Although I've felt like I really was going to die three or four times in the past few years so it does get you thinking."

"You mean like the other night, when we were helping Organized Crime?"

"Yup, like then. I really thought that was it. I couldn't move, I couldn't call out, nothing. It was horrible, and I knew you guys had lost me, I figured I had gone undercover one job too many. It was really weird though ... I was so scared and then I went calm and realized that I was going to sit and wait to die. Nothing I could do but just sit and wait."

She shuddered. She knew she couldn't tell Thomas, not yet anyway. But she thought that eventually she may be able to tell him the story in a funny way to ease some of the fear and so it wouldn't seem so traumatic. She knew he worried too much about her work and especially whenever she went undercover. She didn't want to worry him so telling him would have to wait. There was so much she couldn't tell Thomas. And it seemed like things were piling up ... the shit pile was getting bigger and bigger.

"Man I am so sorry," Robert said, "I feel so bad that you had to go through that."

"Are you kidding," she said, "it wasn't your fault ... and if it hadn't been for you ... I probably would never have been found. I want to thank you again Robert for always being there for me ... always having my back, you know."

"It's my pleasure, and likewise for me thanking you. You always make me look so good."

"Fuck you," Sam punched him.

She smiled. Her mind wandered. Robert was such a good partner for her, she decided. Calm and usually cool and always had her back. It was like she had a big brother. And she was so glad that it was him that saved her that night in the limo rather than one of the other guys. She knew that Robert would never tell anyone about the thong. Small petty detail in life, she knew, but still worth knowing. She didn't even feel embarrassed anymore in front of Robert. At one time she may have, but not anymore. Now she just felt trust.

The radio broke the silence. Barry had been spotted at another truck stop, this one south of Springfield, just north of Litchfield. Robert put his foot down on the gas and they pushed on even faster for another hour.

"Okay," Robert said, "I think this is the place."

They pulled into the far end of a parking lot behind the dormant eighteen wheelers. It was late afternoon but plenty of daylight left for an arrest and the trip back, thought Sam.

They parked and slowly made their way by foot toward the buildings, one on each side of the large trucks. As Sam came around the side of one of the trucks she spotted Barry standing beside the building, watching Robert. She thought he was holding a pistol or possibly a revolver.

She slowly pulled her Glock out from under her jacket and lifted it in Barry's direction. She hesitated, she thought she better call out a warning first. But if he made a move to lift his gun she was going to fire. She aimed.

"Hey asshole," she yelled, "try something."

But Barry didn't raise his gun or even turn toward her. Instead, he surprised her by sweeping to his left and into a doorway.

"Shit," she said as she moved forward to pursue. When she reached the door she stood to the side, gun raised in front of her face. She slowly pushed her head around the doorframe and looked inside the structure. Small hallway, empty. Robert came running up behind her.

"I'll go around the back," Robert said pointing with his gun. He slipped away.

Sam entered the hallway and moved quietly toward the opening at the end. She put her head around the corner and saw it opened into a large workshop. It seemed quiet and empty but she knew that Barry was hiding somewhere amongst the truck cabs. She moved quickly from the doorway into an area behind a large rolling tool box. She poked her head out and listened. Nothing ...

She waited a moment and then pressed on into the room with her gun pointing in front of her by her right hand, left hand guiding her along the close counter without having to look. She waited again when she reached the front of a truck. She bent right down almost laying on the floor looking for feet. Nothing ...

She stood and slowly crept around the passenger side of the truck. She passed the door and continued to the back. Suddenly a sharp pain caught her breath as something hit her full force on the back of the neck. She collapsed, gun flying forward and bouncing on the cement. Barry jumped down from behind the cab and ran off.

What happened? She couldn't think. Wait ... wait ... this can't be happening ... one second standing and in the next on the floor. She couldn't see, her eyes were blurry. Everything spun around and her head hurt like crazy.

Robert ran up and tried to help pick her up off the floor.

"Hey partner, you ok?" Robert asked.

"Fucking hurts ... let's get this bastard." Sam felt around the ground and found her gun under a truck.

They crept further into the workshop around the trucks. As they reached the end wall, Sam noticed a door. She motioned to Robert and they approached from both sides. Robert tried the handle slowly and quietly. It gave way and he signaled. Sam burst through the door with her gun pointing forward but Barry was quicker and grabbed her hand with the gun and threw his arm around her neck. He was about to drag her over to the corner and threaten them both with a shot to her head when suddenly, the grip was gone. Robert grabbed Barry and threw him nearly across the room, into the large shelf. Barry crashed against the shelf and crumpled to the ground.

Sam flopped back onto the cold cement. She tried to focus her eyes. Slowly her vision began to clear and she sat up. Robert had pulled Barry up to his feet and had his hands cuffed behind his back.

Robert walked Barry over to where Sam was sitting.

"You okay? Robert asked.

"Yup," she said, "I'll live thanks. And thanks ..."

"Hey no prob ... That's what partners are for," he smiled and pushed Barry forward through the door. "You're under arrest for being such a fucking dick-head." He pushed him again.

Barry was already in the back of the car by the time Sam found her gun and returned to the vehicle.

"Hey partner, you going to be alright?" Robert asked.

"Just need to sit down," Sam said.

"You hungry?" he asked

They drove to the front of the truck stop and parked.

Sam looked back and noticed the sharp and deadly eyes of Barry staring coldly at her as she climbed out of the vehicle and entered the restaurant.

chapter sixty eight

It had only taken a couple of hours to get back to the precinct and throw Barry into an interrogation room, cuffed to the chair.

When they had first arrived, Director Davis had come out of his office to congratulate them. He asked them about all the details of the arrest.

"I don't want any fuck ups on this arrest," he said, "I want to make sure this asshole goes away for a long time."

Sam sat opposite Barry. Robert was pacing the room from time to time while he asked questions. They had already grilled him a few times but they wanted to keep going over his story until he cracked.

"So let's go over it one more time," Robert said.

"Fuck," Barry said, "I told you, I ran cause I thought you were chasing me for the robberies. I didn't have anything to do with those deaths. Didn't you guys check my alibi?"

"Yah Barry," Robert said, "you're never going to get us to believe you. We did check your alibi and you know what, it didn't wash buddy. It was a shit alibi Barry, you should have come up with something better."

"Yes we looked into it," said Sam, " and we interviewed your mother's nurse, and she agreed you could have slipped out most of the nights and gone back just to make an appearance at the end before you left. It doesn't hold up very well now does it?"

"Fuck you."

"Now Barry," Sam said, "that isn't going to help you, you know. Getting mad at us is only going to make us mad ... and making us mad is only going to get you more problems."

"I want my phone call," Barry yelled.

"See that's what we mean Barry," Robert said, "until we get a little cooperation, I don't think we will be giving you anything."

"Are you telling us," Sam said, "that you ran because you thought we were after you because of a few robberies?"

"Yah I am."

"Well that's not good enough," Robert poked Barry in the chest.

"Okay, okay," Barry said. "It was that and the phone call."

"What phone call?" asked Sam.

"I got a call last night from someone," he said. "He told me I had better run, that you guys were looking for me and going to pin the murders on me."

"Who was it?" Robert asked.

"I don't know, I didn't recognize the voice. It was kind of disguised, you know muffled somehow."

"Just hang tight a minute," Robert turned to Sam. "We need to talk." He stood and led the way out of the room.

"So what do you think partner?" he asked as they stood in the hallway.

"I don't believe him, he's lying," Sam said. "He's making the whole thing up. The guys a fucking serial killer, a psychopathic murderer and an expert manipulator. Have you looked into his eyes?"

"Yah, so?"

"They look evil," she said.

"Could be but I just don't see it."

"All I want to know," she said, "is how he picked the other four after Connie. How did he pick Natalie?"

"Okay let's pry it out of him," Robert said.

They returned to the interrogation room and sat facing Barry. He no longer looked necessarily evil, just mad.

"Are you guys charging me with anything?" he asked. "Cause if not, I want to go."

"It will be at least a day or two before that Barry," Sam said.

"Yah," Robert said, "we just want to talk and get to know you better Barry." Robert smiled. "Now tell us Barry, how did you pick your victims?"

"I was renovating their homes," Barry said, "what the fuck do you mean how did I pick them?"

"No Barry, not the robberies," Robert said, "we meant the ladies you killed ... How did you pick them?"

"I told you ... I didn't kill anybody."

"Then why did you run Barry," Sam asked.

"Oh for fuck sake," Barry said, "I told you I was scared you were going to pin the murder of those bitches on me."

Sam stood up and slapped Barry. One quick backhand slap. Short, sweet and painful. Barry didn't exactly scream, but close. Sort of a schoolgirl's howl left his lips as his head flew sideways.

"You fucker," Sam said between her teeth, "one of those so called bitches was one of my best friends."

"Sorry, I didn't mean any disrespect," Barry said as he straightened up. He tried to reach up and wipe the blood from his mouth, but the handcuffs stopped him.

"Samantha," Robert said, "in the hall ... now." Robert sounded pissed.

Barry was starting to look a little worried now as Sam glanced back at him on her way out of the room.

"What the fuck were you thinking," Robert said, "you heard Director Davis earlier, no fuck ups with this arrest. He wants everything to go as smoothly as possible. He wants Barry put away for life. And now this ..."

She stood tall. "I just lost it, the guy's an asshole. It won't happen again."

"You bet it won't happen again, you have to leave this one to me now ... I have to send you home Sam. I can't have you fucking this case up any more than you did already. I just hope he doesn't press charges."

"Shit. I'm sorry."

"Yah, and he'll probably want to deal down the murders and robberies now that he has something to bargain with. Jesus Sam, go home and get some rest. It's been a long few days and one of your best friends is gone." Robert turned back to the door.

Sam felt terrible. She had never gotten mad and lost it on anyone before.

"Go home and do some grieving Sam ..." Robert said as he entered the room and closed the door.

chapter sixty nine

The smells, the exotic music, the darkness. She pretended that her killer wasn't tired of playing with her. Fear? Struggle?

She adjusted the mask slightly so no vision was possible. Absolute blackness. The intimate darkness. Her erotic darkness. Like every time he had drugged her and bound her to the bed. Perfect darkness ... no need to see. Nothing in the world worth seeing, only the sense of touch, feeling the ultimate pleasure.

She thought about the irony between the night she was in the power of Antonio, able to see but not move or feel anything and all the recent times in her bed not being able to see but feeling everything. She didn't know which would be a worse way to die. Seeing and not feeling or feeling and not seeing.

Her hand brushed her left breast and she brought her fingers together over her nipple. She squeezed it slightly and rolled it between her fingers.

She had arrived home in the late evening sun to an empty, dark house. She had driven around the city for a while trying to clear her head after slapping Barry but it all seemed like a complete waste of time.

And now it was night. She had remembered as she walked in the door earlier that Thomas wasn't going to be home until the next afternoon. Fourteen or fifteen hours away. Long and lonely hours.

She climbed the stairs to her bedroom slowly. She didn't want dinner, she wasn't hungry. She ran the bath instead.

The tub was hot and felt good on her aching body. Her neck hurt from Barry trying to knock her out, she had aches and bruises everywhere from the past few days. Her crotch was slightly darkened in color and had a slight purple hue to the skin where the bruises had been the worst, but at least nothing hurt. She didn't think she had any permanent damage, nothing that time couldn't heal.

She had dried off quickly and climbed into bed naked. She pulled the covers up tight. She lay staring at the ceiling, the shadows from the moonlight changing with the breeze.

What had she done? she thought. Why did she have to ruin it? Hopefully Robert can fix it and get Barry to talk.

Why would Barry do it? Why would he kill Natalie? Did he kill Connie first and then get a taste for death? Did he find the need to kill the other women before or after Connie?

And poor Natalie. What was the point? After everything else in life, and then to be taken out like that, it was just all too cruel. Tears began to form in Sam's eyes and slowly rolled down her cheeks.

She lay thinking for hours, again sleep was no where near, like so many other nights. Without thinking, she got up and opened her underwear drawer and removed the shoebox. She lit 2 candles that were sitting on the bureau and turned on the CD player.

She opened the box and lay back down on the bed. Reaching inside without looking, she felt the mask. She pulled it out along with the vibrator. She slipped the mask over her eyes and immediately felt the familiar dark pleasurable space, along with the smells of candles and the exotic music filling the room.

She tried to relax. She suddenly felt there was so much resting on her, so much pressure in her life, coming from all directions. Her life felt so chaotic, she had no time to slow down and feel happiness. And there was no time for love.

If only Thomas were here, she thought. I can't wait until tomorrow. I just need to crawl into his arms and cry. Cry for Natalie, and cry for the others. He always makes me feel so safe and secure.

Nothing in the world can touch me when I'm with Thomas, she thought. But now I'm alone ...

And that's when her hand brushed her left breast and she brought her fingers together over her nipple. She squeezed it slightly and rolled it between her fingers.

She adjusted the mask slightly so no vision was possible. Absolute blackness.

Then she slowly reached over to the vibrator and turned it on. The sound of the humming was drowned out by the exotic sounds of the music. She lifted it slowly to her breasts and rolled it around one nipple and then the other. It created an amazing feeling, like someone was electro charging each area. Her nipples responded by hardening and every nerve in the area became even more responsive. It was as if her chest was being electrified to attention. She rolled the vibrator between her breasts and left it laying pointing upwards toward her chin as she took both hands and massaged her breasts, fingers pinching and rolling her nipples. Her breathing increased and between her legs became moist. Her body began to tighten.

What more could she do to help Natalie? she thought. She had to nail Barry and she'd even fucked that up. What was Robert going to do? Her body relaxed. Fuck.

She shook out her thoughts and tried to concentrate on her nipples again. She thought of Thomas, if his hands were kneading her breasts, like she was doing to herself. His strong hands working around her nipples.

She slowly moved the vibrator down her lower tummy, down toward her vagina. Her body tightened again as she pretended Thomas was blowing on her navel as he had in the past.

But what if Barry wasn't the serial killer? What if he was telling the truth? Fuck. Her body relaxed again.

But if it wasn't Barry, how could she ever figure out who? What leads did they have? What evidence? What little detail had she overlooked?

She shook out her head. She felt the vibrator reach her clit. Her body tightened as the amazing feeling of electricity started to warm her entire crotch. She rolled the vibrator between her outer lips and touched near her vagina. She held it there as her body began to warn her that soon she would be in heaven.

And how can anyone get over the death anyway. She hadn't even talked with Melanie or Matt yet about Nat's death. How were they coping? Fuck, fuck, fuck … her body went limp.

She would have to call Melanie and talk. I would imagine she knows by now, Sam thought. She's probably heard from Debby by now.

This was her first close death. She remembered her grandparents all passing away, but she was much younger then, and she had felt a further distance from them. And anyone she knew on the force that had been killed, at least so far, wasn't really that close. Even her guilt over the death of the hooker, Angel, wasn't this close. And the other four ladies, although sadness and grief had surrounded her, nothing had prepared her of the feeling of permanence with someone so close. She would never again get to talk with Nat. Never again get to laugh or cry or hug Nat. Never again get to tease her or hear her quirky sense of humor.

How permanent death felt now when so close. Even the times Sam had thought she was going to die, she had never really thought of the permanence. It's one life that we have, she thought, and when it's over, it's over … nothing else … no way of going back and making changes …

She felt the pressure of everything building in her mind again. She was feeling overwhelmed … too much to worry about … too much happening that I can't control … the killings … her secrets that she hadn't released …

And dark thoughts swept into her mind. Deep fears and horrors beyond the bank, beyond the limo, beyond her bed. She felt the curtain rise to her inner most fears, disguised as deep desires all this time. She feared for her life. Not of living, not of dying, but of herself taking her own life. That she realized was her darkest secret, something she hadn't even allowed herself to think before. She was just a little envious of those five women only for a second, but it was there long enough for her to notice. She was envious of their death, their peace, their quiet stillness without the struggling pressures of the world pushing inside their heads from every direction. She was blinded by this twisted envy … her sickest envy … the darkest envy … her dead envy. To shut the world off.

That was it. She could shut the world off. If only she had the guts. If only she had the courage.

She froze. Wait, she thought, wait … wait … I can't think that way …

Focus! Come on, she thought, you have the tools for pleasure in your hands, just use them. Feel the pleasure. Take a moment out of your life to enjoy yourself.

She shook her head. Live for fuck's sake. Think of Thomas. Think of everyone else that you know. Think of yourself. Living is what takes courage.

The vibrator was humming and numbing her crotch in a delicious feeling of such a warm build up. She suddenly felt that she needed Thomas in so many ways. She felt isolated and needy. She felt she wanted him inside her so badly. She reached over and picked up the dildo from inside the box. She placed it between her legs with her left hand as her right hand rolled the vibrator around. She slowly pushed the dildo inside herself.

Oh my God, she thought. The feelings of ecstasy began to take over her body. She tightened, her body arched as she withdrew and pushed it in again. She felt her entire core stiffen in such intense thrilling pleasure. Fireworks were going off in her head.

She felt like she was floating on air, her body was riding wave after wave of body-numbing ecstasy as she moved the dildo in and out faster and faster.

She snatched the mask away from her eyes quickly and turned to the mirror. She watched her own pleasure light up her face. She radiated a naked glow of truth and beautiful elegance.

An addictive drug had taken hold of her brain and she now knew she was clear in thought. She suddenly felt lifted of all her guilt. She realized no one knew her or her inner most desires and thoughts. They didn't need to, she was the only one. She was what was really important to herself. She didn't need to feel guilty for her deci-sions, her actions, her desires, herself. She was just a woman trying to get through life and to be a good cop. Something she liked. And a woman getting through life and needing only to answer to herself. She read her own eyes in the mirror. And her an-swer would be yes, ... yes you will live. And yes you are me. And yes you will be guilt free.

She realized maybe she didn't have all the answers but she at least now knew all the right questions.

And then she came ... and shook violently through her orgasm ...

She was free. She was whole. She was beauty.

chapter seventy

She awoke. The sun was breaking through the edges. The room felt warm and smelled a little of sex.

Life, she thought, my life. She smiled.

She pulled the covers higher up on her naked body around her neck. This time however, not out of fear or shame, but only because she was chilled.

She lay quiet and stared at the ceiling. The haze of last night had lifted from her and she felt a fresh new insight about herself. She felt really alive … she was in love … really in love … and she knew that nothing else mattered. Thomas was hers.

She only briefly thought of Barry and his victims. Of Robert and her own mistakes. She only thought briefly of Melanie and Matt, and of Alex. She would let each thought enter and exit her mind without worry or pressure. They drifted in and out at their own speed.

And then she thought of the hands. Those secret lover's hands of such desires and intense pleasures. The hands that had taught her so many amazing lessons about her body and her real feelings of herself.

She froze. Wait, she thought, wait …
wait … it can't be … the fucking bastard!
The fucking bastard! She suddenly realized
whose hands they really were!

I am going to catch you and make you
pay, she thought … you fucking bastard. I
will now have my revenge. My true revenge
… my way!

She jumped out of bed and threw everything into the shoebox and hid it away. She
showered and drove to the office a little
faster than normal. She was blind in her
quest to find Alex.

chapter seventy one

Sam found Alex at her desk. Monday mornings were usually pretty quiet in the lab and being that early, there was no one around.

"I need another favor," Sam said as she sat down beside Alex's desk.

"Oh," Alex said, "and a good morning to you too."

"Sorry, but this is a rush."

"Okay what is it?"

"Do you have any kind of knock-out drug?" asked Sam. "You know something I could use to knock someone out without harming them?"

"Do I want to ask who or why?"

"I'll let you know soon but I just want to get this done quickly and get it done my way."

"Well, I do have a couple of chemicals that would probably work. But all of them are powders that need to be dissolved in some sort of liquid like water or whatever."

"Okay," Sam said, "that'll work. Can you give me something that will knock someone unconscious for fifteen to twenty minutes?"

Alex led her over to a locked cabinet. She unlocked it and handed Sam a small plastic bottle with white powder inside.

"Here," said Alex, "two teaspoons of this mixed into a drink and he or she will be out like a light for a minimum twenty minutes. But use it carefully."

"Thanks Alex," Sam hugged her. Sam wanted to avoid anyone else that may walk into the lab so she left quickly through the back door.

She decided she had to make arrangements right away. She called Robert from her car while she drove to the mall. She wanted Robert to think that it was his idea she stay home for the day.

"Hey Sam," Robert answered his phone on the first ring.

"Hey Robert, I'm really sorry about last night."

"Don't worry about it, Barry didn't seem too concerned. He's more worried about all the evidence that I told him we have against him. Just take some time Sam, to adjust to everything. I'll cover for you today okay?"

"Thanks a lot Robert, I owe you."

"Hey no prob partner, talk to you later."

When she hung up, she thought to herself, I do not want to be disturbed today. She turned off her phone.

She parked at the mall and found the local beauty salon. She asked them for a total make over, hair, make up and the works. Monday morning was the perfect time to ask. They fit her right in.

If anyone had been paying attention that day, they would have noticed a cop walk in to the salon and a few hours later, an exotic beauty walk out. Her long, dark hair was now pulled up, her dark eyes had three complimentary hues of brown eyeshadow. Her nails and lips a dark shade of red, her smooth skin radiated. She walked out tall and confident, she felt like a beauty queen.

When she got home, her phone was blinking. Someone had left her a voicemail. It may be Thomas, she thought. She called her service and listened to the new message.

"Hey Sam, it's Alex. I was trying to reach you cause I have some crashing news … here it is … remember I told you MacKetchison was really mad at me for helping you out, well he caught me today and made me enter all your DNA samples into our database. I told him more or less how they were illegally collected but he didn't care, we wanted them in the system anyway. Well here's the shocker Sam … one of them matched the killers hair that I processed yesterday. Sample number 20 is the same fucking guy Sam, your serial killer … anyway call me as soon as you can okay … bye."

What the fuck, Sam thought. One of her samples matched the killers? Holy fuck, they might finally have the bastard. But for now she had more pressing things to think about, she had to move on with her plans for revenge.

Sam changed into her favorite sexy Penware panties and bra, and covered those with her favorite red Marlika dress. She hid away Alex's drug in the kitchen and arranged everything for the night.

We are going to do this my way now you bastard, she thought, I will show you whose really in control of this fractured and dysfunctional relationship between me and your hands.

chapter seventy two

Sam slowly put her mouth to his left nipple and her hand to his right. As she sucked and played, he was groaning through the gag. She moved her hand around his chest and up to his neck.

She sat back and moved her hands down to his hips. She dragged her nails across his lower tummy above his penis. He tried to squirm but the bindings held tight. She was going to drive him nuts tonight, she decided. Maybe he would die tonight, just from the extremely pleasurable torture. She had to keep it going long enough to show him who was really in control.

She moved her hands and dragged her nails around his thighs. He groaned again. She wanted to hear him groan all night long, torture him into submission. Win out the contest, own him.

His penis was hard and she leaned over and blew on it. She wanted him to be on the edge of release the entire time.

She had drugged him earlier and carried him upstairs, thankful she was in shape. She had lit candles and turned the exotic music on load. Louder than normal, she wanted him worried. She had bound him to the bed using the same straps and in the same way he had done to her the many times before. Except she didn't leave him the failsafe. No clip attached to a finger to gain his freedom. She put the mask on him to take away his sight, she put the gag in his mouth and then sat back and waited for him to wake up. She wanted him to lay there and ask himself, what kind of a wild animal have I created with my exploring and secretly probing hands ... with all my experimenting, have I now created a monster?

Sam stood and walked over to the bureau. She had a glass of ice water waiting. She looked back at her captive and smiled. He was helpless. He was hers.

She took an ice cube out of the glass and carried it over to the bed. She stood above her prisoner and let the ice drip onto his stomach. He tried to jump but the straps held tight. Sam smiled. It felt so good to be in control.

She sat down on the edge of the bed again and leaned over him. She kissed his forehead twice and sat back. Then she started to rub his stomach and lower abdomen with the ice. Slowly, slowly circling.

He gasped. His hard penis twitched. She knew he was loving this.

You bastard, she thought, you are going to pay.

When the first ice cube melted, she turned her attention and scratched her nails down both sides of his body. She toyed with both his nipples and then squeezed them until they were hard.

She had earlier decided that she wanted to concentrate on her revenge, it seemed more important to her than anything else at the moment. So she had decided to take a night off from work and focus in on the moment of total intimacy between him and her. It seemed that important. Her thoughts had been only for the ice, his penis, his torture, her control. Her revenge.

She sat back and smiled. She wondered if she should take a few photos for black-mail purposes. She would be able to make him do anything she wanted. Absolute control.

She leaned over to lick his penis from bottom to top.

Suddenly she froze. A chill seemed to rip up her back into the back of her neck.

Wait ... wait ... something is wrong, she thought. Wait ... what was it ... the message from Alex. The sample ... it wasn't sample 20 that matched the killer, there was no sample 20. It was sample 02, Alex had done her switching numbers thing again! Holy fuck! That means …

I have to warn Robert!

She stood and leaned over, "I'll be back lover, don't go anywhere …" she whispered into his ear.

She ran down the hall. It was dark now and the moonlight streamed in wherever the windows allowed. She knew the house was dark so it would cover her naked body. She only had to find the phone.

She started down the stairs, blue moonlight mixed with orange streetlights caused the kitchen to be bathed in multicolored strips of dark and light. The rest of the house was dark. When she was near the bottom stair, a golf club hit her across both shins. Thomas's number seven iron was the actual club. The timing was perfect and the club had been swung with enough force to send her sprawling across the front hall and into the far wall. She was knocked out from the hit to the floor before she even crumpled against the wall.

chapter seventy three

She awoke. The first thought that popped into her head was how she had to get word to Robert.

She opened her eyes. She was handcuffed to the stove handle. Her arms held awkwardly above her head, laying naked across her own kitchen floor. What the hell just happened? she asked herself. Who the hell was here?

She heard a door open and light foot steps coming in from the front hall, maybe the front bathroom door? In walked Ron. Director Ron Davis. Multiple murderer Director Ron Davis. Dressed in a full-length, head to toe, black leather body suit with a humorous looking flap covering over his genital area. The suit also had a hood hanging down from the back of the neck with what looked like a mask attached to the hood.

"Hello Dahill," he said.

"What the fuck Ron?"

"Sorry Sam but you were getting too close," he said. "And then you guys found some revealing surveillance tape ... well that was just too much."

"It was fake Ron," she said, "you idiot, we faked the announcement to flush out Cummings."

"Thanks, it doesn't matter to you now though does it?" he said. "But you've saved me some trouble telling me that. At least I won't have to go around and take care of Robert after I've finished with you."

"You'll never get away with it," she said.

"Sure, I just have to stage it the same and no one will even suspect." He held up an open mouth gag. "It will be kind of fun, you'll see."

Fuck, she thought, even if I scream no one will hear me.

"Why are you doing all this Ron?" Sam asked.

"Because I like it," he answered and smiled. "I enjoy seeing someone like you down on your knees in front of me, helpless, waiting to die while sucking me off. I get to hold your head in my hands as you take your last gasps of air while my penis cuts off your breath. I assure you it is one of the most powerful feelings on earth. Seeing every one of you bitches pay."

"How are you picking your victims?" Being a cop it was automatic that she ask. Maybe if I stall him long enough, she thought, someone will come to my rescue.

"You guys are handing them to me. Each victim's name and photo comes up in our system and I can just sit back at my leisure and pick out who I like the look of. And no one ever thought to ask about New York."

"Is all this something to do with your wife?" she asked.

"You shut up about her! Don't you dare mention her again." Ron walked over close to Sam.

"So you think this is going to hurt her?"

Ron knelt down in front of Sam and cupped her right breast in his hand. She shivered as he calmly started playing with her nipple. He reached his right hand down between her legs but had trouble reaching any further as she clamped her thighs together as hard as she could. She was in sort of an awkward position laying partly on her side with her legs together and they started to cramp almost immediately. She didn't care. There was absolutely no way she was going to let Ron touch anywhere remotely close to her crotch area. She held her legs shut as hard as her leg muscles would allow. Ron shrugged and reached up to her breasts instead.

"Relax honey," he said as he kneaded both breasts, "trust me I have no intention of raping you. I just want to use your mouth that's all." He smiled.

"Fuck you," Sam spat in his face.

He slapped her hard once in the face as he wiped away her spit. Then he calmly said "I'm just about ready for you, okay? Now you don't go anywhere will you ... just hang around for a bit okay?" He laughed. He stood and went back into the front bathroom.

Wait ... wait ... something ... what was it ... something was trying to get through her thoughts.

Something was pressing into her head with a dull ache ... Houdini ... that was it ... Harry Houdini ...

Sam looked up. She twisted her hands once counter clockwise and then once clockwise quickly. Click, she was free. She jumped up and ran over to the shadows beside the kitchen entrance.

Ron walked out of the bathroom. This time his hood was up over his head and a mask surrounded his eyes. Only the lower half of his face was visible. He walked back into the kitchen and stopped. He hesitated at the doorway only for a moment trying to adjust to the empty stove and a missing Sam.

She hit him hard in the stomach from the side. He bent over slightly, the leather deflecting most of the blow. He put up his hands and stepped back in the same move causing Sam's next punch to miss its mark. He swung around and with his back toward her, punched his right elbow back hard into her chest.

She crashed back into the kitchen table. She steadied herself and stepped forward throwing a couple of quick punches toward his face. The first one he blocked with an arm but the second one caught him squarely on the chin. He fell backward into the hallway but managed to stay upright. He kicked out and caught her right thigh. Her leg gave out and she started to fall toward him. She threw her arm out and caught the doorway to stop the fall. He punched her with a quick right jab to the stomach but she turned and it hit her on the side. She pushed off of the doorframe quickly and threw another right to his head. It caught him on the cheek and he stumbled back further into the front hall.

"You are one tough son of a bitch Sam, I'll give you that," Ron said through his teeth.

I have to keep hitting his face, she thought, his leather suit is protecting everywhere else. She was trying to remember all the moves that the boys had taught her and she had practiced over the years. She even had some moves from the street crud that had come in handy in the past.

Moonlight sparkled off of her sweaty body as she turned and kicked fast trying to hit his shin but he stepped back and blocked her foot. Hoping that's what he would do, she was already moving down and tucking into a roll. She came up with her left hand grabbing at his right hand where she clamped on and with her right arm directed at his face, she pulled him into her punch. He went down hard grunting.

"Fuck you," she said.

She stood above him and waited. She knew he wasn't finished. He slowly rolled over and when he tried to get up she kicked him hard in the chest. He flew onto his back and slid toward the front door. Sam relaxed slightly and looked around for something to tie Ron up with. But Ron had other plans and sprung up quickly.

Fucking leather suit, she thought. He moved quicker than she anticipated and punched her hard in the chest knocking the air out of her lungs. As she went back she caught herself on the wall and tried to straighten up. But he punched her again quickly in the stomach before she could react and she went down hard onto her tailbone with a crunch.

He picked her up off the ground by her neck with both hands and threw her hard backward into the kitchen.

Sam flew back over the kitchen table and into the bottom cupboards by the sink. He walked over and slowly picked her up by her hair. He punched her once in the stomach and twice in the chest. Then he held her up and hit her hard in the face. She flew back into the counter with a thud and collapsed forward onto the floor.

She knew she was done. She couldn't even lift her arms to protect herself. Fuck. What could she do, no one was there to protect her. No one there ...

chapter seventy four

Sam lay in the middle of the living room floor. Ron had dragged her naked body by her feet out of the kitchen and into the living room. He explained to her slowly that he was about to turn her over and tie her wrists together with a shoelace he had found in the front closet. He wanted her to know each little step that would lead to her violent death. He spelled it out, he was going to sit on the couch while holding her mouth over his penis, while she took her last breaths. He held up a pair of her nylons he had found in the laundry basket by the hall. He smiled as he reached down to push her over.

She knew at that moment it was her only hope. She knew instinctively that she had just enough left in her body to commit to the move. She kicked out with her right foot as fast and as hard as she could directly into his throat. His eyes showed surprise as he fell back into the couch slipping to the floor in his leather covering. Sam tried to lift herself up to run but Ron grabbed from behind and pushed her into the small table by the edge of the couch. The same table that held a drawer where

Sam sometimes left her primary gun when she was in a hurry or just too lazy to lock it away upstairs.

As she hit the table her hands immediately went to work opening the drawer. She flew through the table and onto the floor, Glock now in her hand.

Ron stood up quickly throwing his arms up in order to pounce, golf club in hand. That's when she fired the first shot. It slowed him as it burst into his chest, but not as much as she liked. The second and third shots seemed to slow him enough as he slipped down onto his knees and dropped straight forward. Dead before he hit the ground. She knew. She didn't even have to double check, she could see it in his eyes.

She sat for a moment and took a couple of long breaths. She knew what she had to do but she just wanted to delay it as much as possible. She sat quietly and stared at her enemy. Death stared her back.

She stood up very slowly, pain coming from places she didn't even know existed. She found the portable phone in the kitchen and called Robert.

"No rush Robert," she said, "he's not going anywhere."

Then she ran upstairs into the bedroom. She climbed onto the bed. Candles still lit, music still blasting. She massaged his penis, it was still half hard. She climbed on top and straddled him. She slipped his penis into her and began to pump her body up and down slowly. She was really going to enjoy this, she decided, and this time she was in control. She leaned over and undid the gag and pulled it from his mouth. She then tore off the mask.

The smiling face of Thomas looked up at her. He looked delicious.

"Is everything okay?" Thomas asked.

"Perfect," she smiled, "but we only have six or seven minutes before all hell breaks loose."

"I love you Sam," Thomas said.

"Fuck you, you bastard," she said and then she kissed him deeply.

Visit
http://www.dead-envy.com

Look for Detective Samantha Dahill
in the next two Chrissy Deker thrillers:

DEAD LOVE - coming early 2014

and

DEAD LADY - coming mid 2014

Contact Chrissy Deker or
check out her story at:

http://www.chrissydeker.com

www.ingramcontent.com/pod-product-compliance
Lightning Source LLC
Chambersburg PA
CBHW070319030726
47505CB00004B/1025